A Monkey in Office

Page 62

Frontispiece

A
MADCAP BROWNIE

BY

SIBYL B. OWSLEY

Frontispiece by Andrew Wilson

BLACKIE & SON LIMITED
LONDON AND GLASGOW

Printed in Great Britain by Blackie & Son, Ltd., Glasgow

A MADCAP BROWNIE

CHAPTER I

Moppy's Scheme

" Mum! Akela says——"

" Oh, this Wolf Cub jargon," groaned Daddie, jabbing his garden fork into the hard soil.

The little boy in the green cap and orange scarf had been tumbling over himself in his eagerness as he rushed home from his Wolf Cub parade. Now he jerked his head back in sudden silence.

His mother left off spraying her rose trees and held out a comforting hand.

" What does Akela say, Wriggles?" she smiled.

Wriggles darted towards her.

" He's been telling us what we shall w-want for camp," he stammered. " Three blankets and a b-blacking brush and a mug and a knife and——"

" Do be quiet, Wriggles!" burst out Moppy, his

ten-year-old sister. She flung back from her face the thick brown curls that gave her her nickname.

" I'm sick of Akela," she began.

" Leave Wriggles alone," defended Daddie. " I was only laughing when I groaned. We hear plenty about your Brown Owl. Why shouldn't we hear of Wriggles' wise old Wolf?"

" What does he want to talk about camp for when it's not yet June?" grumbled Moppy.

" Looking-glass forward," teased Daddie. " Where's your Brownie smile, Moppy? Left it in your bath?"

Moppy flushed; then she darted off in shame to the baby pine wood by the side of the house.

She was always losing that Brownie smile now. No one knew it better than herself, and she was dreadfully sorry about it.

Moppy skidded down among the slippery pine needles, and sniffed up the scent of the pines while she thought things out.

It was this camp business that had started her scowling. Everybody must see how ridiculous it was. Here was she, Moppy, very nearly eleven years old, and here was Wriggles not quite ten; and Wriggles could go to camp and she couldn't.

Why should Wolf Cubs be allowed to camp and Brownies not?

It was a riddle to which Moppy could find no answer, and she hated not finding things out.

And everybody knew that Moppy was clever. And Wriggles was all jerks and eagerness, so jumpy that he could never keep still. Moppy was always the leader when they played together.

It just wasn't fair.

And it was more than two whole months to camp, and for more than two whole months Moppy would have to listen to Wriggles panting out his excitements.

Supposing her Brownie smile never came back for all that time?

Moppy went plop down on the ground at such a dreadful thought.

What could she do to get it back?

At that moment two children's voices drifted over the hedge into the wood.

" Iris and Ann," recognized Moppy.

A sudden scheme shot into her head. The beam it brought was big enough to break into half a dozen Brownie smiles.

" Hi! you two! Wait a sec!" she shouted, and darted to the little gate that led into the lane.

Iris and Ann both belonged to Moppy's Brownie Pack. Iris was the Elf Sixer. Moppy and Ann were Elves, too. Privately, Moppy thought she would make

a much better Sixer than Iris, but Brown Owl had not
even made her a Second. Moppy felt sorry for Brown
Owl for not being a better judge, but she didn't bear
her a grudge about it. She merely gave the Six the
benefit of her quicker wits. Iris did not always say
" thank you ", but Moppy shut her eyes to that.

Iris's little sister, Ann, ran to Moppy and put her fat
little arms tight round her waist. Ann loved Moppy, and
always showed the whole of the untidy gap that her missing front teeth had made when Moppy came in sight.

Iris looked a little prim.

" You know the Wolf Cubs are camping at Urchin
Bay, don't you?" cried Moppy.

Iris nodded.

" You've got a cottage there, haven't you?"

" Um-m," beamed Ann. " We go there drekly
school's over."

" Do ask me to stay," begged Moppy.

" *Yes!*" stressed Ann.

" Why?" asked Iris.

" I want to be there when the Wolf Cubs are camping," cried Moppy. " I thought we'd have a camp of
our own. Anyway, we'd have adventures. We'd show
them what splendiferous things girls can do. It's
ridiculous that Brownies can't camp. You will ask
me, won't you?"

" I'll see what Mummie says," answered Iris.

Moppy didn't mind one scrap asking herself. She knew that Iris's daddie had lots more money than her own, so that it couldn't possibly matter having one extra. Why, Iris had a whole shilling a week pocket-money, while Moppy only had sixpence. It didn't seem to make much difference, for Iris put most of hers into a money-box. Moppy did think that was silly. She loved the feel of spending.

Very often her sixpence was spent on other people. She didn't mind that one bit, as long as she could spend. But Iris was soon going to fly up to the Guides and she knew a Guide must be thrifty. Moppy always thought that was the one Guide Law that was foolish.

Iris didn't very much want Moppy to come and stay. Moppy so often got one into mischief. But Mrs. Pritchard, Iris's mother, thought that Iris was a little too tidy and good.

" Let her come," she decided. " She'll ruffle my chick's feathers and make her twice as lovable," she laughed, as she tucked Iris up in bed.

CHAPTER II

Work for Moppy

" Let me put the signalling flags away, Brown Owl!" begged Moppy.

" Very well," said Brown Owl.

Moppy quickly collected all the flags but two. A tiny Brownie was still struggling to roll hers evenly round their sticks.

Moppy took them from her.

" I'll do it for you, Vera," she said.

" No, Moppy, it's kinder to let Vera learn," corrected Brown Owl.

" Very well, Brown Owl," sighed Moppy.

There had been an enrolment that day, and Brown Owl had gone through the Brownie Promise with her Pack.

Moppy was thinking it over as she strolled home.

' The keynote of the Brownie promise is obedience,' Brown Owl had told them. There were times when Moppy liked to forget this, so she hurried her thoughts on.

' Do my duty to God and the King.' Moppy had loved that part too. She was a daring little soul, ever ready to fight a battle for the things and people she liked.

She wished she had lived in the time of Charles I. Moppy knew quite a lot of history. She was very fond of it. She liked making up plays and pageants from it for her and Wriggles to act.

A funny little smile came over her face. Why, it would have been Wriggles who would have fought for Charles, not she! Wasn't it queer that Wriggles always had to be the one to do all the things that she was sure she could have done much better? But Moppy felt quite loving towards Wriggles again now that her camp scheme was shaping, so she generously allowed him the honour of fighting for his King.

" I would have buckled on his armour and kept his sword bright for him," she told herself. " And I would have hidden him from the Roundheads down a secret passage and brought him food and been ever so brave," she chuckled.

All that was much more exciting than the dull meaning Brown Owl had put to the 'King' part of it that afternoon.

Being loyal to one's King just meant being a good citizen, she had told them. And in case these little people did not know what this meant, Brown Owl had gone on to explain that being a good citizen was only doing everything they had to do just as well as possible.

" I'll do something first hand for the King, see if I don't," decided Moppy. She was so eager about it that she actually said it out loud.

A tall thin man who was passing caught the words. He gave a hard laugh.

" You'll do something for the King, but you'll pass misery on the road," he mocked.

Moppy pulled up startled. She was too young to understand his words, but she felt she was up against something hostile.

" Wouldn't you do something for the King?" she challenged.

" Can't do anything for my own kid," retorted the man. " Look here, youngster, I've a little 'un at home. She's younger than you, but she's had rheumatic fever. She's a poor wee thing, and it's left her heart bad. She can't play games like other children, and she's only got one doll that's so old she's rubbed its face away, and I've no money to buy the food to make her plump and well, let alone to get her playthings. Makes one bitter, that does."

Moppy felt terribly sorry for this unknown child.

In fact, it made her feel quite choky. But she did want this poor man to be friends with the world as she was.

" Have you asked anyone to help?" she demanded.

" Not me. It shouldn't be necessary," muttered the man.

Moppy grew red with perplexity. Then she burst into speech.

" The King would be dreadfully sorry if he knew. He does everything he can for everybody," she declared. " But he just doesn't know. It's like Wriggles when he sprained his ankle last winter. He limped home a whole mile and made it awfully bad. Lots of cars and carts passed him, but he wouldn't ask for a lift. He just stopped while they were near so that the drivers couldn't see he was limping. He had just been hearing about Captain Scott and his last journey to the South Pole. He wanted to see if he could endure things too. Mummie and Daddie told him he was very silly, and so he was. That sort of endurance did no good to anybody. Can't you see that the drivers were not unkind? They just didn't help him because they didn't know."

Then suddenly Moppy gave a little sob.

She stopped aghast at herself.

The man looked down at her worried face and smiled quite kindly.

" Bless the kid! It's only words! I didn't mean what I said. I've lots of wounds on me for King and Country. And I'd get them again if it'd help," he confessed.

" But your little girl isn't only words, is she?" whispered Moppy.

The man shook his head.

" Do tell me her name," she begged.

" Betty Horpe," conceded the man.

" Where do you live? May I bring Betty some toys? May Mummie make her some soup?" pleaded Moppy. " I'll run right home and tell her now!"

But Moppy did not run very far. Round the corner was waddling the most terrifying creature she had ever seen.

It was only a mild bulldog, but Moppy had never seen a bulldog before, and this one was ugly enough to have won a first prize. Its great teeth were gleaming in the sun; and, to Moppy's ignorance, its jaw seemed jutting out with malice. It seemed hardly possible that this hideous creature and Wisp, their own perky, laughing fox terrier, could both be dogs.

Her battle of words had left her rather trembly. She did not want any more strange encounters. She cast her bravery to the winds and ran back to the unknown Betty's father.

It was probably the unknown Betty that made him so clever at understanding. He even took her to her home, crushing her hand in his rough one.

As they parted at the gate it was the usual sparkling Moppy that faced him.

" I've got lots of schemes in my head for Betty," she cried. " I expect the King works through his subjects, don't you? He shows us what he likes done, and 'specs us to do it whenever we can. That's being a good citizen, don't you think? And I dare say he'd just as soon I did something for one of his subjects as for himself."

It did not take Moppy long to enthuse the whole family over poor little Betty.

Mummie visited the cottage that very evening, and brought with her not only soup, but a kindliness that radiated like sunshine through the house.

The next day she took Moppy.

Moppy's best Brownie smile soon wore away Betty's shyness.

" I believe you could be a Brownie, you know," exclaimed Moppy. " I must ask Brown Owl about it. Which would you rather be? A Pixie, a Gnome, an Elf, or a Fairy?"

Then, seeing Betty's big blue eyes grow bigger than ever with bewilderment, she tried to tell her more clearly of the wonderful Brownie magic that can flood a fairy brightness over the humdrum things of every-day.

The two mothers stopped in their talk to listen.

Moppy's brown curls kept tickling Betty's pale face as she bent eagerly over her. Betty's mother looked wistfully at Moppy's pink cheeks. Then she smiled bravely.

" Oh, well, there're white roses as well as red, aren't there?" she challenged.

" I'll come again awfully soon," promised Moppy as she left.

Before her next visit, Moppy and Wriggles routed out their toy cupboard. Wisp, the fox terrier, helped. It was a task he rather enjoyed. There was generally a ball or two to be found, and a few things like dolls' brooms that he particularly liked to prance about with. But for Moppy and Wriggles the result to-day was hardly satisfactory.

Moppy had never cared very much for dolls, and, in her latest historical pageants, it had been the more bloodthirsty episodes that had held sway. The remainder of the dolls had died a glorious death as Lady Jane Grey, the more unfortunate of Henry VIII's wives, and as Mary Queen of Scots. There was not one that they felt would be an improvement on Betty's own. And Wriggles's clockwork train and meccano sets were thought to be inappropriate.

Moppy inspected her money-box. Three forlorn farthings, too insignificant to spend, were all it yielded.

For the first time she thought enviously of Iris's heavy one, a fat pillar-box almost too full to rattle.

She put her own feather-weight one back on the mantelpiece and faced the situation.

" We must earn money, Wriggles," she decided.

" Wouf!" agreed Wisp. Then he leapt excitedly at Moppy's curls.

He may have been tired of staying indoors on a summer afternoon. But Moppy put another meaning to his impatience.

"The darling! He's offering us his hoard," she cried.

For Wisp was a very clever dog. He was awfully good at catching, and sometimes people would throw him pennies for fun. He had been taught to run off with them to a baker's and buy buns. But sometimes, when he'd had an extra good dinner or the weather was very hot, he would hide them in his basket instead. Just as he would bury a bone against a rainy day. Daddie said he liked to lie on them and dream of sticky buns.

Moppy stooped down for him to put his paws on her shoulder.

"Darling Wisp," she murmured, "course we won't take your hoard. Not even for Betty. It wouldn't be playing cricket. Would it, Wriggles? But thanks most awfully, all the same. Now, whatever can we do?"

"There are our gardens," suggested Wriggles. "P'raps we can sell our mustard and cress and our pansies. And I've got some lettuces too."

But Moppy often forgot her garden in the many schemes that chased through her brain. It had not been watered and weeded and hoed like Wriggles'. It did not yield such a harvest.

"I could only get the teeniest bit of money from mine," she sighed.

"Then there's groundsel," continued Wriggles. "Lots of people want it for birds. We can find quite a lot. And there's some among your weeds, isn't there?"

Moppy nodded. It was nice of Wriggles to find some use for her weeds.

"I'll go and garden this minute," she exclaimed, snatching up a baby spade.

Wisp went too. He was very fond of digging, though Daddie said he always dug in the wrong places.

"Why don't you use your paws?" he barked out at

Moppy. "They're much quicker than a spade. See what a hole I'm making!"

But Moppy's thoughts were too full of Betty to notice Wisp's remarks.

For five minutes she pulled up and dug with an almost dangerous vigour. Then her eye caught something shining in the sun. She pounced upon it eagerly. It was sixpence.

"I wonder if Daddie dropped it. I must ask him," she thought. She slipped it into her overall pocket and started to dig afresh.

Again a gleam caught her eye.

"Another sixpence! How queer!" she laughed, and put it to companion the first.

But that was not to end her findings.

Again and again did the gleam of a sixpence call to her.

The fifth time she gazed at it in astonishment. "It can't be Daddie, it's a treasure trove," she cried.

At the sight of the sixth, she gave a whoop of joy.

"I know! I know! A Bank must have been here once. I shall find thousands of sixpences buried!" She left it on the ground and flew off to Wriggles to tell her wonderful news.

"I've dug into a mint of money! We'll take Betty

to the sea. We'll give her Devonshire cream till she bursts!" she cried.

Wriggles gazed a little sadly at his sister. What a wonderful Moppy she was! Always doing clever things. . . . Then he thought of what it would mean to Betty, and flushed with joy.

" Moppy, you are s-splendid," he cried.

" My pocket's bulging with sixpences," gloated Moppy.

" Is it?" asked Wriggles doubtfully.

Moppy patted it triumphantly.

Then she stopped, dumbfounded.

The pocket was quite flat and soft.

She thrust an earth-grimed hand inside.

Not even one sixpence remained.

She stared at Wriggles in horror.

" L-look, there's a hole," stammered Wriggles.

There was indeed. The tip of an investigating finger was already showing through.

There must have been one sixpence there at first. It must have kept dropping through.

But sixpences did not often dwell unknown in Moppy's pockets. She thought it over.

Ah, yes. She remembered now. Mummie had told her to buy some stamps that afternoon, and she had thought so much of Betty's toys that she'd forgotten.

It was so dreadfully disappointing that she felt all dull and tired. It was quite a long time before she could even go back to her garden to pick up that one horrid sixpence.

When at last she did so, she gave a little cry of surprise.

Lying in the middle of the path was her discarded weeding basket. In it was a lovely warm brown egg. A strange hen must have scuttled in through a hole in the hedge and laid it there.

" Do you think I might count it mine, Mummie?" asked Moppy, when Mummie came home.

" I think so," smiled Mummie.

" Then I shall have a present to take Betty after all."

On her way to Betty's cottage, she met Iris and Ann.

" Where are you going, Moppy?" demanded Ann.

Moppy told them. She also told them about the tragic sixpence.

" I've lots of money in my money-box," cried Iris. " Couldn't I get her something?" she begged.

Moppy grew red. She had so wanted to be Betty's fairy godmother.

Then she flung back her curls in scorn at herself.

" Of course you can. It'll be lovely for Betty," she cried.

CHAPTER III

Moppy visits her Brown Owl

In the daytime Betty had a bed by the kitchen window. Daddie brought her down every morning, blankets and all. Her big blue eyes saw Moppy coming even before she lifted the latch of the gate. By the time Moppy's sun-browned legs had skipped up the cobbled pathway, Betty was all ready to welcome her with a trembly smile, and with two bright spots of colour on her usually pale face.

" Come in!" she called out, in answer to the rat-tat of Moppy's knuckles on the cottage door.

" Hulloa!" beamed Moppy.

" Hulloa!" whispered Betty.

Her breath was coming very quickly.

Her mother stopped in her ironing to look anxiously at her little daughter.

" Steady, don't get too excited now," she warned.

" Can't Betty get up?" asked Moppy. " It must be dull for her."

" Not yet. See how she's panting even lying in bed. Her lips are quite blue sometimes. Still, she'll get up soon, the doctor says."

" And then she can come down to our Brownie meetings; we'll teach her all sorts of things," cried Moppy.

Betty's mother shook her head.

" She's to go slow for ever so long," she said. " Even when she is up, she can only look on at things, not do them for quite a bit."

Moppy sighed. It would have made her and Wriggles perfectly ill only to look on. She stared at Betty's wistful face. It was like a triangle, she thought. Broad at the top, with its high cheek bones on which the pink of excitement still lingered, and such thin little cheeks tapering down to a pointed chin.

" I'd like to make your face round like this," she cried, bunching up her own in her brown hands.

That evening Moppy was very quiet. Instead of doing homework, or romping with Wisp, or playing cricket with Wriggles, she just mouched about the garden.

" I'm seeing what it's like to do nothing," was all the explanation she gave.

" I *wish* Betty could be a Brownie," she exclaimed

suddenly, kicking quite viciously at the rubber ball that Wisp had hopefully brought to her to throw.

"I *wish* she could be a Brownie. I *wish* she could go to Urchin Bay," she burst out.

"If wishes were horses then beggars would ride," disposed Daddie, who had just finished a hard day's work and was settling down in a deck chair to read his paper.

"Wishes can be made into horses, if one wishes so hard that it makes people *do* things about it," cryptically and ungrammatically announced Moppy. "I'll go and see Brown Owl."

Daddie put down his paper and watched his little girl dart off.

"There's something in that daughter of ours besides bumptiousness," he told Mummie.

"She won't be so bad when she tones down," admitted Mummie, with a smile.

Brown Owl lived at the Rectory. Her father, Canon Chesney, was working in his garden in his shirt sleeves. Moppy flung herself in at the gate with an energy that creased his kind lean face into smiles.

"Shouldn't mind you as a partner, Moppy! I think you'd get things done," he laughed. "Want to see Brown Owl?"

"Please," beamed Moppy. Like everybody else

she loved this rector who had only come into the country when long years of battling with the ugliness of London slums had carved his face into deep furrows.

" He looks so stern and he is so kind," Moppy had once told her Daddie.

" Stern to sin, kind to the sinner," Daddie had summed up.

Moppy had not understood, but she had remembered.

Canon Chesney gave a long soft whistle. It was the signal by which he often called his daughter.

She quickly appeared. She was not very tall, but slim and nut-brown. Her dark eyes were rather like a dog's in their steady seriousness, and her hair was glossy and straight.

" You make such a lovely Brown Owl," Moppy had told her.

" Hulloa, Moppy!" she exclaimed, "there's no Pack meeting to-night."

" I know, Brown Owl. But I just couldn't wait for the proper day. Drekly after last Pack meeting, I had a most wonderful adventure."

Brown Owl looked wary. Adventures had a way of swarming round Moppy like wasps round a honey-pot. But they were sometimes not adventures of which Brown Owl could officially approve.

" This is an adventure you *must* know about, dear Brown Owl," pleaded Moppy. " I'm sure you can help."

Then out tumbled the story of Betty, her rheumatic fever, and her bad heart.

" She's longing to be a Brownie. I've told her such lots about our Pack. I thought until this evening that she could be one of us drekly she could get up. But her mother says she must only look on for ages. And that sounds horrible. Don't you think you could persuade her to let Betty come to our meetings once she's out of bed? I'm longing to teach her R-r-rats and Rabbits, and Shipwreck, and all our lovely games."

" She wouldn't be strong enough for a long time," decided Brown Owl. " But I've a finer idea still. One which will let her be a Brownie right away. She won't even have to wait to be out of bed. Look on? Of course she shan't look on. She shall do and be, just like any other little girl."

" Oh, Brown Owl! How?" cried Moppy, dancing up and down in excitement.

" She shall be a Post Brownie."

" A what?"

" There's a Brown Owl who writes lovely letters by post to invalid children who want to be Brownies. It's most awfully exciting for them. There're——"

" But then Betty wouldn't belong to us," interrupted Moppy. " And I did want her to."

" Indeed she would," corrected Brown Owl. " A Post Brownie joins an ordinary Pack too, just like any other Brownie. So Betty can join ours, of course. She can even belong to one of our Sixes."

Moppy brightened. " She can be an Elf, can't she?" she begged.

" I dare say," smiled Brown Owl. " We'll make her feel she's really and truly one of the Pack. I will visit her and get her through her tests, and you can all help, for little girls of her age are too young to learn things only by post. And besides all this, she will get her lovely monthly letters from her Post Brown Owl. You can't think how nice they'll be. And they'll have stories and competitions in them as well. So, instead of feeling out of all the things that the Brownies can do, she will be almost more in them than you."

" How absolutely ripping! And I should just think we *would* help," cried Moppy. " I can go in almost every day, and Iris and Ann will love to visit her, and so will——"

" Not so fast, you impetuous monkey," checked Brown Owl. " Mrs. Horpe'll like her cottage to herself sometimes, remember. She won't want to be tumbling over Brownies at every hour of the day. The

Pack must only visit its Post Brownie with me or Tawny, or the Pack Leader. That's a rule, you know. It's to prevent eager little people from becoming worries instead of helps."

Moppy's face grew blank.

" But Brown Owl! Betty's my friend. I simply must go and see her alone sometimes. And I think Iris is going to be a friend of hers too," she added loyally. She could guess how disappointed Iris would be if she were prevented from taking her the presents that she felt sure would be the outcome of that fat money-box. And she knew Iris would not want to give them in the presence of everyone else.

" What are we to do about it?" she cried.

Brown Owl smiled down at Moppy's disturbed face.

" Of course, if you're real friends as well as fellow Brownies-to-be, that makes a bit of a difference," she admitted. " You must talk things over with Mrs. Horpe. If she likes you to visit Betty unofficially, then of course you can."

Moppy's eyes again began to twinkle. " And anyway, she's not a Brownie yet. I'll get in as many visits as I can first," she challenged mischievously.

Brown Owl laughed. " You'll have to be quick then," she retorted. " I'll go and see Betty myself to-morrow, and if she really wants to be a Brownie,

I'll write to the Post Brown Owl in the evening. Post Brown Owl will have her registered right away."

" Brown Owl, you're a *duck*," declared Moppy.

" How can an Owl be a duck?" objected Brown Owl.

Moppy grinned delightedly. Then she once more grew grave.

" But supposing her mother and daddie say ' No '?" she asked.

" They won't when they understand," reassured Brown Owl.

Moppy heaved a sigh of relief. It all sounded so lovely. Even Wriggles' camp seemed a small thing when compared to this glorious change that was to come into Betty's life.

" Do you want to tell the Pack yourself, Brown Owl?" she asked wistfully. " For I'm just longing to talk about it. I—I don't know that I can keep it in till we all meet."

" Very well," laughed Brown Owl, " I won't be cruel and ask you to do the impossible. Say what you like."

" *Darling* Brown Owl," cried Moppy, " I'll go off this very minute and tell Iris and Ann."

" You'll go off this very minute to home and bed," contradicted Brown Owl. " That's where Iris and Ann are, I know. And asleep too, probably."

Moppy sighed. Why did her days always come to an end long before she had crammed into them all the things she wanted to do, she asked herself?

" Then I'll start off to school awfully early to-morrow morning and go and meet them," she declared.

Moppy and most of her friends went to a jolly day school called Rushmoor. Lots of her school-fellows were fellow Brownies.

Moppy could hardly wait to finish her breakfast the next morning, she was so anxious to spread the splendid news about Betty.

She was so early starting off that she had to dawdle about the lanes ever so long before she caught sight of a school-fellow.

As she had hoped the first two she met were Iris and Ann.

They seemed to be walking terribly slowly. And Moppy decided that she had gone far enough out of her way.

" Come quick! There's lots to tell you!" she called out, as she stood on the grass by the side of the road and signalled her impatience.

" Betty can be a Brownie. But it's a specially lovely kind of Brownie. The sort that little ill children can be. I'll tell you all about it as we go along."

" How do you know?" questioned Iris the precise.

" I asked Brown Owl if she might. I went and saw her last night. I just couldn't wait for the Pack meeting. You don't mind, do you, Iris? But it seemed so dull for Betty."

" Oh, Moppy, you are wonderful!" cried Ann.

" Oh, Moppy, I *am* glad!" whispered Iris. " Mummie's going to take me to see Betty to-day. We're going to buy a lovely doll. She can't have that just at once, as Nannie and I want to dress it. But the doll's to be quite new, and a baby one. I thought Betty would like to feel nobody had been its mother before she was."

Moppy had never seen Iris quite so excited about anything. Her eyes sparkled so that she didn't look one scrap prim. Moppy felt very fond of her.

CHAPTER IV

Betty's World Widens

Brown Owl kept her word.

The very next day she visited the Horpes and found them all at home.

She was wise enough to tell them at once that she was a friend of Moppy's. That made them welcome her.

Then she explained to Mr. and Mrs. Horpe how happy it would make Betty to be a Post Brownie.

" Brownies are such useful little people too. You won't know your house when you've got a Brownie in it," she laughingly told Mrs. Horpe. " Betty's going to be an Elf. Here's the rhyme that belongs to her Six:

> ' This is what we do as Elves,
> Think of others, not ourselves.' "

" All the thinking in the world can't make Betty

useful while the poor little thing's on her back," sighed Mrs. Horpe.

" Nonsense," retorted Brown Owl. " Aren't there things to darn?"

" Lots," agreed Mrs. Horpe, gazing hopelessly at her pile of mending.

" Brownies learn to darn," smiled Brown Owl. " And don't you sometimes wish you had someone to remember for you?"

" Just don't I?" sighed Mrs. Horpe. " What with taking in washing and doing a day's charing when I can, I keeps forgetting half the things I should remember."

" Brownies like memory games," hinted Brown Owl. " And it's wonderful how a Brownie smile shortens the day."

The end of it was that Brown Owl produced an exciting sheet of printed paper to be signed by Mr. Horpe and the doctor. And it was not to say that Betty was too ill to attend school or any of those horrid things that make it so clear that one is ill and poor. It said instead that Mr. Horpe agreed to Betty being a member of the 1st Comfrey Hill Brownie Pack, and that her doctor guaranteed that she was not suffering from any infectious disease.

Betty almost burst with pride and importance.

A few days later she felt more important still.

"Mummie, the postman's coming up the path!" she cried suddenly.

Mrs. Horpe wiped her hands on her apron and hurried to the door. Postmen did not often come to their cottage.

"A letter for the little 'un," smiled the postman. He thrust a cheery red face inside and nodded at Betty.

"Oh!" gasped Betty. She twisted the envelope this way and that quite in awe. Never before did she remember getting a letter by post.

"Open it!" laughed Mrs. Horpe.

"Mummie, it's from my Post Brown Owl!" she cried. "And look! there's a picture tumbling out too. Why, it's a Brownie and a Wolf Cub fighting the funniest little dragons."

"There! how kind of the young lady!" exclaimed Mrs. Horpe. Real tears of gratitude were in her eyes as she saw the joy on Betty's face. "Shall I read you the letter, dearie?"

"Course not. I can do it myself ever so easy," declared Betty. And indeed she could. Post Brown Owl had written her welcoming letter in such big clear writing that it was as easy to read as print.

"Sit down, Mummie, just here by my bed and listen." begged Betty.

" DEAR BETTY,

(" See, Mummie, she knows my name and all!")

" DEAR BETTY,

" I am so excited to hear that you are going to be a Post Brownie—another little person added to my large family. I think I must have nearly as big a one now as the old woman who lived in a shoe. Only I'm not like her one bit. I never say I've got so many children I don't know what to do. I just want more and more and more of you. My shoe has elastic sides, you see. So it'll stretch and stretch and hold all the little girls who want to be Post Brownies.

" Now that you are a Brownie, I expect you would like to have a little corner or treasure-box of your very own in which to keep all your Brownie things. I am sure that Mother will give you one if you ask her."

" Will you, Mummie?"

Mrs. Horpe nodded. " Go on," she said.

" Here is a pretty picture to put in it.

(" We've seen that, you know," reminded Betty.)

" Would you like to learn the Good-night song that all the Post Brownies sing before they go to sleep? These are the words. The chimes of Big Ben:

> ' O Lord our God,
> Thy children call,
> Grant us Thy peace
> Until sunrise.
> Good night.'

" You sing them to the tune of a clock chiming the hour. And ' Good night ' is like the two first strokes of the hour itself.

" What a lovely surprise it will be for Brown Owl if you can sing it to her when she next comes to see you!

" You will get a letter from me in July. It will have stories, pictures, competitions, and all sorts of lovely things in it.

> " Lots of love,
>> " From
>>> " POST BROWN OWL."

Betty lay back on her pillow in absolute content, and started to read it once more quite to herself. So intent and happy was she as she clutched her letter that she did not hear Moppy scampering up the pathway. She did not know she was there at all until Moppy's brown curls thrust themselves between her and her letter.

" I thought you must be asleep!" cried Moppy.

" I've had the loveliest letter from my Post Brown Owl. You may look at it if you like," conceded Betty.

Moppy did so. She chuckled and nodded her head approvingly as she read.

" I 'spec she's nearly as nice as our Brown Owl," was her verdict.

" *Quite* as nice," corrected Betty.

" That's a lovely song to sing every night. It looks ever so easy to learn," declared Moppy. " And I've so many things to teach you, I don't know where to begin. Yes, I do! We'll be patriotic and start with the Union Jack. What do you know about it?"

" It's red, white and blue, and crosses," said Betty vaguely.

Moppy surveyed her from heights of inutterable superiority.

" There's lots more to know about it than that," she laughed. " I expect it'll seem a bit mixy at first. But I'll teach you with paper flags next time I come. Brown Owl showed us how to make them and fit them on to each other. You can do it too."

" I should love to," beamed Betty.

Moppy produced a stumpy pencil and a grubby piece of paper from her pocket. " I'll begin to teach you to-day, though," she proclaimed.

" First we had St. George's flag—a red cross on a white ground like *this*:

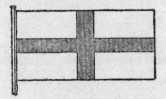

" Then, when Scotland joined England, we had to bring in St. Andrew's banner. That's where the blue comes in. St. Andrew's cross is white, but it goes corner-wise, so:

" St. George's went on the top of it with just a little bit of its own white. That was easy.

"But Ireland gave an awful lot of trouble when it came in in 1801. St. Patrick's banner is red and white too, like St. George's, only his red cross is corner-wise like St. Andrew's.

"If they stuck it on as it was it would quite wipe out St. Andrew's. So they did such a funny thing; they cut St. Patrick's cross in half, and kept just a little white with it as they did with St. George's."

"I see," interrupted Betty. "They showed half of St. Patrick's and half of St. Andrew's."

"It's not nearly as easy as that," regretted Moppy. "A flag flies from a staff, doesn't it?"

"Um," vaguely agreed Betty.

"Well, they put the lower half of St. Patrick's cross near the staff, and the upper half on the side farther away."

"Whatever for?" questioned a rather bored Betty.

"To show that St. Andrew's came first. If you fly the flag the other way it's all wrong. All the same, I like the stories about St. Patrick best. I'll tell you the one about him where he was a little boy in the winter. He had a poor foster-mother, and she lived by a river. It was an awfully tiresome river. It overflowed in the spring and froze in the winter. One day when it was very cold St. Patrick had gone with the other children to the woods to get sticks for the fire, but the icicles were so long and glittering that he broke some off from the bank and ran home with them.

" His foster-mother *was* angry. She was shivering with cold, and I 'spect the icicles made her feel colder still.

" ' Why didn't you bring faggots that I might warm myself?' she told him.

" Then dear little St. Patrick looked at her ever so gently and this is what he said:

" ' Believe in the power of God and the icicles should flame.'

" Then he threw the icicles on the dying fire and they turned into warm, glowing logs."

" How nice!" agreed Betty.

" I can tell you lots more," continued Moppy.

But here Mrs. Horpe interfered.

" Betty's brain'll be fair addled if you don't go slow," she declared. " Off with you now, Missy, or I'll tell that Brown Owl of yours you can't have no private visits."

At which terrible threat Moppy fled.

The next morning, of course, there were more excitements to tell Iris and Ann. Once more she set off far too early for school, and awaited them at the same grassy patch.

" Betty's had such a jolly letter from her Post Brown Owl," she announced. " And I've begun to teach her her flags."

" How jolly for her!" exclaimed Iris. " And oh, Moppy, I've been longing to tell you something, too! Mummie thinks that by the end of July Betty will be strong enough to come and stay with us at Urchin Bay. Don't you think it would be awfully nice to have her?"

Even Moppy, chatterbox though she was, could find no words to express her joy at this wonderful treat.

" Oh, Iris," she gasped at last, " it was my very secretest wish. I had just longed for it to come true. But I wasn't a fairy godmother, so I didn't see how it could. Oh, *aren't* you excited?"

Iris was. But, being Iris, she still remembered that there was such a thing as school to be reached by nine o'clock. So she restrained the delighted war dances of Moppy and Ann and hurried them on.

CHAPTER V

The Reign of Terror

" Iris Pritchard, come here!"

Frances Butterworth, the school's second tennis champion, stood in the doorway of the Junior cloak-room and commanded.

Iris left off struggling with a rebellious shoe-lace, and came to hear her senior's bidding.

" I want you and some other kid to fag for us this afternoon."

Iris's face fell. Frances was not popular with the Juniors. She was a girl who took no notice of little ones unless she wished to make use of them. Besides, Iris was due to play in a rounders match for the Upper Second. Still, Sixth formers had to be obeyed. Iris sighed, but nodded.

It was unfortunate for Frances that she should have chosen to descend on the Juniors on this morning when Moppy was feeling so all-important and so extra friendly with Iris.

All unwitting of the thunder in the air the Senior continued to stress her command.

" Now, mind! Two-thirty sharp, and another kid with you. Don't forget!"

But this insistence was the undoing of Frances. Before she had left the cloakroom a spitfire of a Moppy had hurled itself in her path.

" You would drop on Iris, wouldn't you?" jeered the atom; " you would choose a girl who wouldn't cheek you You'd be afraid to ask *me*—I know!"

" Moppy!" gasped her milder companions.

" How dare you speak to me like that, Muriel Lorraine!" gasped Frances.

A nervous titter rippled round the cloakroom. Of course Moppy's name was Muriel, but no one ever thought of her as anything but Moppy. It did sound queer.

Moppy, prancing first on one foot and then on the other, executed an elfin dance of defiance in front of the Senior.

" Get your rotten Middle School to fag for you," she cried. " We're not supposed to have anything to do with the big building."

Nor were they. Rushmoor School proper was an old foundation, which stood in the most ancient part of the town, in the same square, and of the same age, as the Parish Church, which held tattered fragments of standards so old that there was nothing left of them but shreds. There had been no room to build on to it when modern hygienics had demanded more space for its scholars. So the Juniors, very important, had decamped to the jolliest house of their own. Here the top girl of the Upper Second found herself a power instead of an insignificant babe. The discovery had been so brain-reeling that, although the first head girl of the Junior School had now a real baby of her own to play with, even the Juniors of to-day had not quite recovered their balance. They still suffered from " swollen head ". There was a lot to make them, too. The school proper had been built at a time when playing fields had not been thought of. Its hockey and tennis grounds were a modern addition quite close to the Junior School. The Juniors, on the other hand, possessed a beautiful garden. Here, quite independent of the Senior sports ground, they could play their rounders and learn the rudiments of tennis. Altogether they were a self-contained, self-satisfied community.

As a rule, therefore, it was the Middle School that provided the great ones with their fags. To-day, however, the Middle School was playing a rounders match. Now, rounders at Rushmoor was not a thing you played at picnics. It was a very serious game indeed. Rushmoor and the other schools round it belonged to a Rounders League. It was a great ambition to come out top of one's league. The excitement over this match was intense. No Middle School girl would have dreamt of absenting herself from it.

" Why doesn't the Middle School fag for you, 1 say?" persisted Moppy.

" They've a rounders match on," vouchsafed Frances.

" And so have we!" cried Moppy. " We can't spare Iris; she's the best thrower-in we've got, and there aren't nine decent players in the Upper Second without her. We're not going to be beaten by the Middle Second to please you, so there!"

If Frances had been wise, she would have caught up that absurd little bundle of fury under her arm; she would have tossed her in the air, given her a good-humoured whipping, done anything, in fact, to demonstrate to her and her open-mouthed fellows how small she was, and how mighty the Senior. She would have shown how laughable it was to see a mouse defying a lion. Instead, she made a fatal mistake. She lost her temper; she growled a threat about order marks and reporting, and walked away.

" We've frightened her—we've frightened her! She's afraid!" triumphed Moppy.

This wasn't true. Frances was merely so angry that she could not trust herself to stay. But her retreat had a most uplifting effect on the Upper Second. The first two lessons were peaceable. They were with Miss Masters and Miss Webb, two of their own Junior mistresses, who were always treated with wholesome respect.

After that came " break ", and with it the divulging of Moppy's idea.

Every fine morning at eleven, out tumbled the Junior forms into the garden ready to mix for play and jabber.

To-day, however, Moppy herded her form down to a favourite wooded corner.

" Go away, you little ones," she told the Firsts and the Middle and Lower Seconds, who were scampering around. " We have things to discuss."

The aristocracy of the Junior School, having rid themselves of smaller and less intelligent fry, held their debate.

" Girls," proclaimed Moppy, " I've an idea. People are afraid of us." She drew herself up to her full length, wished that her mother had not clad her in socks, and surveyed the fellow members of the form. " We will establish a Reign of Terror."

She looked round the group again. Most of them

were wriggling, some with glee, one or two from nervousness. A "Reign of Terror" sounded frightening, even for those privileged to start it.

"What do you mean, Moppy?" asked Iris.

"We won't learn any lessons we don't want to; we'll do just what we like," chuckled Moppy.

"How?" demanded the form.

"We'll frighten the people who come to teach us."

"We couldn't frighten Miss Webb."

"Or Miss Masters," said doubting voices.

"We shouldn't want to," retorted Moppy; "I said we'd do what we liked. We'd like to frighten Miss Whittle!"

"Oh, *yes*!" chorused the group.

Poor Miss Whittle was a hapless science mistress, who had that term arrived at the Senior School, and was next term departing from it. She was very clever, but she had not learnt the knack of keeping order. "Science is such a difficult subject to keep order in," she would bewail. "You must let the girls talk a little when they're working together at experiments. It's so difficult to know where to draw the line." And as it was so difficult, she didn't draw it at all. It was unfortunate for the reputation of the Senior School that this should be the only mistress who came from it to teach the Juniors. It confirmed them in their belief that day that Seniors and Senior staff were a weak-kneed lot whom it was easy to terrorize.

It was at this stage of the discussion that Miss Masters, their form-mistress, appeared on the scene.

" Listen, children," she said, " I'm going off very early to-day, as my mother's come to see me. Miss Harris is very kindly going to give you the last two lessons instead of me. I've written all your home-work quite clearly on the other side of the blackboard. Be good children and win your rounders match."

She had gone and she had left consternation behind her. Miss Harris was Second Mistress at the big school; she had never taught them before, but she was under-stood to be alarming.

" We shan't be able to play tricks on her," mourned the children. " And the Upper School won't think we're terrors, after all."

" Why not?" demanded Moppy. " We've done for the Second champion; we'll do the Second Mistress!"

It sounded terribly brave even to say so. But there was Miss Whittle to practise on first, so hopefully the Upper Second made its way to its classroom.

Science visited the Junior School as nature study.

The subject chosen that day was the dispersion of seeds by the wind. It was a pleasing subject with which to begin the Reign of Terror. Dandelion clocks were prominent amongst the specimens. So much to the good. It was splendid fun to blow dandelion clocks into the face of your neighbour. It was even more fun to catch the winged darts as they floated into the air and, if you missed your capture and upset a form mate or two in pursuit, that added to the glory of the reign.

Miss Whittle's words, as she gave out information from her raised desk, failed to carry as far as the fluttering wings of the dandelions. At first she tried to regard the uproar as the usual unruliness that, as she had told her headmistress, must always accompany a lesson in science. Soon, even she, over-patient and over-dense as she was, realized that it was something more serious. If it had been possible she would have thought that these babies with their socks and sturdy brown legs and diminutive skirts had planned to upset her lesson.

It was a horrible thought. She tried to pull herself and them together.

" Children!" she cried.

She was not even heard.

A bell stood on the desk. If that were sounded it must attract attention. Should she strike it and give order marks to the ringleaders? But there did not seem to be a ringleader. All, even gentle Iris Pritchard, were revelling in their Reign of Terror. To give order marks to a whole form was unthinkable. So the uproar merrily grew.

Then, almost without knowing it, Miss Whittle rang the bell.

The children stopped, surprised in the midst of their frolics. But no one was afraid. Those who administer a Reign of Terror do not feel it themselves. Even those who had wriggled with nervousness at break, were wriggling with glee now.

" What have you got to say? Be quick about it, for we're busy playing." That was what Moppy's face expressed from her cocked eyebrow to her pointed chin.

" You are being very naughty, and I can't possibly go on with my lesson," quavered Miss Whittle.

" Who wants you to?" laughed Moppy.

" For the next ten minutes you can just sit quietly in your desks without being taught," went on the mistress.

They should have been ashamed, but they weren't. They should have sat there getting more and more hot and uncomfortable as the mistress stayed deadly quiet in her desk. Any other day they would; but now they were beside themselves with excitement. " Another victim," gloated Moppy. The class rippled with delight. Iris, who would not have hurt a fly, weakly wiped her eyes with laughter.

Miss Whittle pretended to polish her glasses.

And then twelve o'clock struck, and the science mistress made way for Miss Harris.

" Now, then!" whispered Moppy, and shot encouraging glances in case any heart should falter.

The Second Mistress walked to her desk.

" Shut the door," she said.

No one moved.

The Second Mistress looked in surprise at the Second Form.

They were grinning like twenty little Cheshire cats. Some impishly, some defiantly, some uncertainly.

" Shut the door," she repeated.

Moppy pirouetted towards it, caught the handle as she twirled, and gave a resounding bang.

Miss Harris put on her glasses to take stock.

" Are you trying to be naughty, by any chance?" she asked.

The form tittered.

And then the order marks that might have been given by Miss Whittle descended upon their heads.

CHAPTER VI

The Terrorists Subside

By really enthusiastic terrorists twenty order marks might be considered as trophies pointing to their valour. So the class still forced itself to smile.

" You will all come back for preparation this afternoon," said the Second Mistress.

" Please, Miss Harris, it's a half, and we're playing a rounders match," said Moppy, strangely polite for a terrorist.

" It *was* a half, and you *were* playing a match, you mean," corrected Miss Harris.

Moppy glanced quickly at the Second Mistress; she seemed a very unequal foe for a little girl in socks. She gave up the struggle.

And then the lesson began.

" Quelle heure est-il?" coolly asked Miss Harris.

" Douze heures," chirruped Moppy, still with would-be pertness.

Miss Harris withered her and passed the question on.

" Douze heures," faltered the next three children. They looked appealingly at the clock on the mantelpiece. Its hands were at twelve. Why could not Miss Harris look there if she really wanted to know?

Miss Harris ignored clock and glances.

" Iris!" she snapped.

" Il est midi," stammered Iris.

Colour leapt to the cheeks of the backsliders as they realized the howler they had committed.

The Upper Second had considered itself rather good at French. Before that lesson was finished it felt that the veriest baby in the Lower First must beat it.

It was dreadful the questions Miss Harris asked that day. With uncanny skill she seemed to hit upon all those where a straightforward answer was the wrong one, and the children floundered deeper and deeper in a bog of ignorance and fright.

" Le combien sommes-nous?" she asked the class.

Moppy brightened up. She gave a quick glance round her form-room, counting heads as she did so.

" Nous sommes vingt," she brought out triumphantly.

Miss Harris met her effort with steely silence.

" Vite!" she demanded of Moppy's neighbours.

Lips were bitten but not opened.

" It's awful!" half sobbed Moppy to herself. " And it's awful for Miss Masters too. Miss Harris'll think she's taught us so badly and she hasn't, only we've got so muddled up."

Once again it was Iris who knew the answer. But she gave it miserably. She hated to excel where her schoolmates failed.

" Le neuf juin," she faltered.

Miss Harris looked her contempt at Moppy.

" Quel âge avez-vous?" she asked. Only an eight years old could be justified in such ignorance her voice seemed to imply.

" Je suis dix," stammered Moppy, then burst into tears as she realized that again she had made an unforgivable fault.

The class looked at each other in horror.

Moppy in tears! Then what about them?

" Sn-sniff," came from Iris.

" Sn-sn-sniff," came from nearly all the form.

Miss Harris smiled. She had caught a badly concealed sniff from Miss Whittle as she had passed her.

" Now for some dictation," she said cheerfully.

" Anyway, we'd rather write than speak when we're sniffy," thought the form.

" Collect the papers and bring them to the mistresses' room, Muriel," said Miss Harris later.

Moppy looked up in dismay. Her eyes were red and swollen. She *couldn't* show herself before Miss Webb like that.

" You heard what I said," repeated Miss Harris.

Miss Harris had been in the mistresses' room five minutes before the papers appeared. Even then, Moppy had not succeeded in banishing the red.

Miss Harris's back was turned to her when she entered. She was discussing things with Miss Whittle, who had just finished a more successful botany lesson with Middle Two.

" Why didn't you give them all order marks at once?" she was saying.

" Oh, I couldn't!" objected Miss Whittle. " It would have been so dreadful for them, poor babes."

And as Moppy was feeling a very poor babe at that moment she was grateful. She looked up at Miss Whittle as she handed Miss Harris the papers. Miss Whittle had red eyes as well as she.

The lump in Moppy's throat grew larger.

" Please, Miss Whittle, I'm very sorry," she said, and fled from the room.

When she got back to her form she faced them bravely.

" I say, all of you, I don't think we'll carry on with the Reign of Terror; I'm afraid it wouldn't be very successful with anyone but Miss Whittle; and I don't think I want to bully her any more," she admitted.

" I'm so glad," cried a penitent Iris.

" All right," agreed the others.

" It's a pity you didn't think that before though," grumbled someone; " it's rotten about the rounders."

" Oh, don't grouse!" cried Moppy.

She marched straight to the cloakroom and thrust her curly head into her panama hat before one of her class had appeared. She was ashamed and wanted to be alone.

CHAPTER VII

A Monkey in Office

As a sobered Moppy walked out of the school grounds she tumbled upon Ann.

"How beautifully early you are, Moppy! May I walk home with you?" cried Ann, and, slipping her chubby hand into Moppy's, she skipped along, pouring out the tales of a happy school morning.

"Why, Mops," she broke off to exclaim, "your Brownie badge is undone. How lucky I saw it! The poor Brownie was tumbling off."

Moppy crimsoned as she put up her hand to fasten it. Like many keen Brownies she liked to wear her badge when not in uniform.

She was not sure that the Brownie wasn't really tumbling off and leaving a boggart in its place. She, whose business it should be to make people happy, had made someone so very unhappy that morning that even now it made her hot to think of it. It would take a whole mountain of good turns, she felt, to bury that disgrace.

What would Brown Owl have said if she had known?

But Ann, all unaware of Upper Second escapades, was busy with other discoveries.

" Look, Mops, there're crowds of people by the station. Whatever can be the matter? Do let's go and see!"

Moppy needed no urging. Comfrey Hill, the small country town on whose outskirts she lived, was not a busy one, and in the middle of the day its station was generally nearly fast asleep. Now a throng of jostling curious people were clustered round it, talking and laughing promiscuously.

Moppy and Ann crossed over.

It was not in the nature of Moppy to hang on the outskirts of anything. Clutching Ann's hand she edged her way into the booking-office.

" Oh-h!" cried the two children, as they gasped with delighted surprise.

Seated behind the booking-clerk's grill was a small grey monkey. His wizened face was a picture of queer triumphant glee. He was jabbering softly to himself as he rested his head on his skinny hands and surveyed the laughing crowd.

Then he suddenly stretched out one of his lean arms, rummaged amongst the clerk's pigeon-holes, and produced a pile of tickets. He threw them, as humans had often thrown monkey-nuts at the Zoo, amongst the fascinated crowd.

He flung one with a particularly knowing look right at Moppy's feet.

Moppy stooped and picked it up. It was to Biddam, a village some twelve miles away. And the monkey had not been half-hearted in his present. It was a return ticket.

Moppy's eyes twinkled with mischief. Every re-morseful memory had vanished in the flood of a new idea. Other people had picked up tickets. Some had returned them to the bewildered booking-clerk who had joined the crowd of spectators the other side of his grill. All were remaining grinning in their places. Let the stick-in-the-muds stay and watch if they liked. Moppy was made of different stuff. The monkey had thrown this ticket specially to her. Well then, she would use it. She looked at the station clock. There was a train in five minutes, she knew. They had had a maid once who had lived at Biddam before she married. On her afternoon out she had always been allowed to leave at dinner-time to catch this particular train home.

Moppy fingered her ticket curiously. It looked somehow different from any ticket she had had before. A light dawned on her. It was a whole grown-up ticket, and not a child's. And she and Ann were only halves. They could both travel with it, of course.

She nudged Ann, who was still gazing open-mouthed at the monkey's antics.

" The darling's thrown me a grown-up ticket. I'm going by train with it. Would you like to come too?"

Ann gasped at the glory of the adventure.

" Oh, Moppy, yes!" she cried.

All unaware that one was never allowed to travel with an unstamped ticket, the two children went boldly on to the platform.

Fortunately for them the collector never asked to see their tickets. Moppy was a friendly little person whom everybody knew. She frequently went to the bookstall to change a book for her mother. It never struck him that this time she was a passenger.

Once in the train Moppy carefully divided her ticket.

" I'll put the return in my pocket right away," she announced. " I'll keep the other in my hand to have all ready."

The train was very slow. It stopped at every station, and the guard had friendly talks with the country porters. And in between it crawled. Many people would have groaned at the time it took to do those twelve miles. But neither Moppy nor Ann had ever travelled before without a grown-up. They had chosen an empty carriage, and everything was a joy. It was such fun to lean out of the window without being told to take care of the smuts from the engine, and to dash from one window to the other when a more exciting view appeared, without having to be careful of other people's toes. In one of Moppy's dashes the half-ticket she was holding was jerked from her hand, and floated gaily out of the window.

" Never mind," she laughed. " The return half's safe. If I show them that they'll know I must have had the other."

Her friendly smile was quite enough to convince the Biddam porter.

" All right, Missy," he nodded, just glimpsing the return.

Up to now everything was pleasing them, so that they quite forgot to remember they had had no dinner.

But, when they had left Biddam Station and had walked over a quarter of a mile along the hot dusty road that it opened into, Ann gave a deep sigh.

" I'm drefly hungry, Moppy," she confided. " And they're having peas and strawberries for dinner at home. I know, for Cookie told me."

Moppy sighed too. She herself had discovered she was hungry just a minute ago. She had so hoped that Ann wasn't. " Anyway, I won't say a word," she had just been telling herself. " P'raps she won't think about it."

" I won't mind about the peas, Moppy, if you just get me some sticky buns and ginger beer. Those fill up, don't they?" said Ann bravely.

But Moppy had already felt in her pockets. She knew they were quite empty except for a grubby hanky, much used that morning, a broken penknife, and her return ticket.

" I haven't any money," she blurted out.

Ann gasped. She had always looked upon Moppy as so wonderful and so full of resource that it had never struck her as possible that Moppy should be unable to produce that most imperative of needs, a midday meal. She looked so solemn that Moppy hardly recognized her as Ann.

Once again a quick wave of shame surged over Moppy.

Ann was so small—she shouldn't have brought her. It was horrid to feel hungry. She rather thought she was a rotten Brownie. Well, anyway, she could keep her Brownie smile. On her own face, yes. But could she on Ann's? She would try hard, at any rate.

" I say, Ann," she began, " I know you're hungry. But it's really rather fun, isn't it? We can pretend we're on a desert island, and all the time we know we can always go home, for we've got our return ticket. Look!" And she displayed the piece of cardboard with the precious red band that stood for home and Mother, and food. " Look, Ann," she insisted, " isn't it a lovely thing to have? And when we get home they'll kill the fatted calf—and, of course, peas and everything go with that," she added, with vague hopefulness. " A desert island's awful fun when you can get off it, isn't it, Ann?"

She peered anxiously at Ann's face for a glimpse of the Brownie smile.

Whether Moppy could have brought it back unaided was very doubtful, but just at that moment they turned a corner and came upon a sight that seemed like a miracle.

By the side of the road was a small baker's cart. It had evidently met with an accident and had been abandoned. Tumbled on the road around it were a medley of bread, pork pies, jam puffs, and cakes.

Ann gave a squeal of delight. She creased her face anew into its usual smiles and dimples and ran towards it.

Moppy shamelessly forsook her desert island and followed after.

" Of course they couldn't be sold after they'd been in the dust, could they?" she questioned a ruffled conscience.

"Wait a minute, Ann; let me break off the dusty flakes," she protested, as flashes of hygiene entered her mind.

Then, having thus satisfied her scruples, she and Ann sat by the roadside and ate, and ate.

"Raspberry jam, too! My favourite," murmured Ann, as she munched.

CHAPTER VIII

Other Brownies

' I've had enough," purred Ann at last. But she did not say it while there was a single jam puff remaining to be eaten.

Then she got up and shook and stretched herself like a well-fed kitten.

Moppy looked at her and laughed. There might be no puff left, but there seemed to be jam everywhere.

Ann's dress was smeared, her knees were smeared, her fingers were rosy with it, her mouth was redder than ever.

" Well, you're just the same," retorted Ann.

" Let's go across the fields. We'll find a stream and wash," decided Moppy.

They scrambled over a stile into a meadow starred with ox-eye daisies, and shaded their eyes searching for any trace of water.

" Aren't those rushes there at the bottom? I believe there's a river or something," cried Moppy. " Let's race to them."

They tore down the field.

As they neared the spot two disapproving Brownies suddenly emerged from the rushes. One had the armlets of a Sixer.

" Don't make such a row," begged the Sixer. " You'll frighten all the birds. Don't you know they're sitting on their nests?"

Moppy and Ann stopped abashed. Before the spotlessness of the familiar brown uniform they grew very conscious of their jaminess.

Then the Sixer's glance fell on Moppy's badge.

" But you're a Brownie too," she exclaimed.

Moppy nodded. " Just once to-day I wondered if I wasn't a Boggart instead," she confessed.

Ann's eyes opened wide. Moppy a Boggart? Moppy of all people to be talking of herself as one of those horrible creatures that made every Brownie huddle up close together in the pow-wow ring lest they should slip in through a gap and spoil things!

" Don't listen to her," burst out Ann. " She's the most wonderful Brownie. We should never have had a Post Brownie if it hadn't been for Moppy."

The strange Brownies looked puzzled.

What's a Post Brownie?" they asked.

Moppy and Ann stared in pity at their ignorance. They quite forgot that a week ago they had been ignorant too.

Moppy's momentary diffidence vanished with her new importance. She flung back her curls and forgot her jam.

" Don't you know what a Post Brownie is?" she queried unnecessarily. " She's a little girl who's not strong enough to be an ordinary Brownie and come to Pack meetings, so she has a special Brown Owl who writes to her by post, and the Brownie Pack near her adopts her. It's lovely for everyone. You must have some ill little girl roundabout. Why don't you find her and tell her she can be a Brownie?"

The strange Brownies were so interested that Moppy and Ann loved them at once.

And then, when they had explained everything that they could about a Post Brownie and had told them about the monkey adventure, Moppy and Ann discovered that, though their new little friends knew nothing about Post Brownies, they knew quite a lot about water-birds and their nests.

" Just before you came we had found a nest that a moor-hen had left for a tiny bit while she went off for a change of air," the Sixer told them. " Daphne is going to describe it for her Golden Bar. We'll show it you if you like."

They led Moppy and Ann along by the rushes and yellow irises.

"Do you see how carefully she bent the reeds over it to protect it before she went off?" whispered the Sixer. She did not want to be noisy in case the mother should be coming back. "Isn't it a ducky solid little nest? She must be a very careful mother. Some of them don't make very sturdy houses for their children, Brown Owl says."

Moppy and Ann peeped in. There were five eggs. Such big ones for a small hen. They were white with jolly red splashes.

"You frightened a darling little sedge-warbler off its nest when you came racing down the field," regretted the Sixer. Then, in spite of her own efforts for quietness, she gave a skip of delight.

"There's Brown Owl coming along with the rest of us. We'll take you to her," she cried.

"We've found two Brownies, Brown Owl," she called out, as they drew nearer.

"In a nest amongst the rushes?" laughed Brown Owl.

"No, a monkey gave them tickets, and please, Brown Owl, may we have a Post Brownie?"

Brown Owl stared at the ragamuffins in the steady fashion that Brown Owls have.

" Suppose you explain," she suggested.

Then the Sixer and Daphne and Moppy and Ann poured into the ears of the Brown Owl their own individual versions of Betty and of the monkey.

It would have been clearer perhaps if one of them had told the tales alone. But Brown Owl was clever at fitting in jigsaw puzzles, and she knew that each bit had its own value, so she let them exhaust themselves with chatter. At the end she turned her steady gaze on Moppy.

" So your Pack's adopted a Post Brownie?"

Moppy nodded emphatically.

" I discovered her," she pronounced.

" So you feel she's extra specially yours?"

" Um-m!" agreed Moppy.

" Then I suppose you're the Brownie she will extra specially take as her model?"

Moppy beamed. " I 'spect she will," she agreed.

" That must be a great responsibility for you," observed Brown Owl.

Was it? Moppy stopped in her beam and considered. She hadn't thought of it that way.

" I feel quite sorry for you, you know; you must have to be so very careful what you do if you know there's someone ready to copy you."

" Most of us copy Moppy," put in Ann. " It isn't only Betty."

" Worse and worse," sighed Brown Owl. " *Poor* Moppy!"

Moppy coloured. She rather fancied Brown Owl was laughing at her if not something worse.

" I suppose your people know you've come to Biddam?" she asked.

Moppy shook her head.

" And you took this wee Brownie with you without her parents knowing?"

" How could they? It was the monkey," lamely excused Moppy.

" They must be very anxious," said Brown Owl sternly.

" It's all right, we've got a return ticket," mumbled Moppy.

" Which wasn't paid for," commented Brown Owl. "And, anyway, there's not a train for a couple of hours, and it's a very slow one. Your parents can't go on worrying themselves ill till then."

" We're going back by train," said Moppy obstinately.

" So you may, but I shall telephone first. Do you know your number?"

Moppy nodded and gave it.

" Come along, Pack, we must shorten our afternoon so that I can get home quickly," stated Brown Owl.

Moppy and Ann silently watched the Pack collect its belongings. Brown Owl was ignoring the runaways, and the Pack, versed in the ways of its Brown Owl, gathered that it, too, was to send them to Coventry. Only Daphne and their friend, the Sixer, dared to show dumb sympathy.

" All ready, Brownies?" finally asked Brown Owl.

Moppy took a sudden step towards Brown Owl.

" Please," she gulped, " it doesn't matter one bit about me. I—I can play about till the train goes. But c-couldn't you take Ann back with you and give her some tea? She doesn't like being hungry——"

" I shall never be hungry again," announced Ann fiercely. " I had tons of jam puffs and a pork pie, and I want to stay with Moppy."

" She must be dreadfully thirsty," pleaded Moppy. " And I think that's worse."

Naughty Brownie and reproving Brown Owl eyed each other for a whole minute with equal steadiness.

Then a dimple showed itself in Brown Owl's cheek.

" Come along both of you," she decreed. " Anyway, I suppose you must be cleaned up for the sake of the Brownie brooch."

She gave them tea, and she kept them in her charge

until she saw them into the Comfrey Hill train, but she took all pleasure out of their journey home by throwing away their precious return half and buying perfectly ordinary tickets for Moppy and Ann.

" You are not to send me back the money," she told Moppy. " It'll make you feel uncomfortable not to, I know. But that will help you to remember that little people generally are uncomfortable when they do things that are not quite fair and square."

CHAPTER IX

Moppy returns Home

" Our mummies will come to meet us, won't they, Moppy?" inquired Ann anxiously, as the sleepy little train drew near their own station.

She was remembering that she had set off for school before nine that morning. It was past her bedtime now, quite seven o'clock, and she had not had a glimpse of Mummie all that time! Jam puffs and excitements had made her head " all heavy and funny ", and she was beginning to feel that, much as she loved Moppy, it would be rather nice to be fussed and cared for by someone " quite old " like Mummie.

" I expect so," said Moppy. But she did not feel so comfortable about meeting her mother as Ann did about seeing hers.

One couldn't scold a mite like Ann very much for being taken off by a superior being like Moppy, and, anyway, Ann's family would be so glad to get her back that they'd just want to eat her up with love. Moppy knew those Pritchards. They did kiss such a lot.

But Moppy was old enough to know better. The strange Brown Owl had rubbed things well in before she had parted with Moppy that evening.

Still, Moppy did want to see everyone quite badly, even if she did get a first-class scolding, so she rushed with Ann to the window, and stood looking out over Ann's head as the train steamed into the platform.

Yes, there was Ann's mummie and daddie and a clean shining Iris, all waving as hard as they could wave with forgiveness smiles on their faces. But Moppy couldn't see her own family anywhere.

They absolutely hadn't come to meet her, though they must have known she was arriving, for it was they who had passed on the message to the Pritchards.

A great lump came into Moppy's throat. Hadn't they cared, then, when they thought she had been lost?

And by this time Ann had been swallowed up by her adoring family, and Moppy was left, feeling very small and not at all important, on the platform alone.

" Ticket behind," Moppy heard Mr. Pritchard say, as they bundled Ann past the ticket collector.

She slowly gave up the tickets Brown Owl had given them. There seemed no fun about the expedition any longer. She caught sight of a contented Ann being whizzed off in the Pritchards' car, and started to trudge home alone.

Suddenly she grew alert.

How hard someone was running behind her! And listen! Wasn't her name being called?

She looked back. Wriggles, his usually pale face scarlet with exertion, was dashing after her.

" I d-did w-want to be in time," he panted. " B-but I had to take a m-message for Dad."

He hitched an arm over Moppy's shoulder.

" W-wait a sec, old thing," he begged. " It is decent to have you back."

Moppy tried to produce a smile. It was a dismal failure.

" I can't ever be a really truly Brownie now, can I, Wriggles?" she whispered huskily.

" Oh, I don't know. King David fell, and the Lord loved him," cheerfully announced Wriggles.

Unlike Moppy, Wriggles's favourite subject was Scripture. " It's much nicer than history, Moppy," he would argue. " For God can do everything, you see. It makes it so exciting. You never know what's going to happen next." And this knowledge that with God all things were possible, had a way of helping Wriggles to do things that his rather timid nature could never have done by itself.

But the thought of David failed to comfort Moppy. She knew that David was chosen of the Lord. Now, as a rule, Moppy had a very good opinion of herself but it was not that sort of opinion. She was quite aware that she was an independent little scamp who brought about her own misfortunes.

So, once Wriggles had regained his breath, they walked along in unusual silence.

Unusually, too, it was Wriggles who broke it.

"Moppy, dear!" He said it nervously. There was clearly something very much on his mind. "Moppy, dear! Mummie and Mrs. Pritchard went down to the school when you and Ann didn't come home. S-some of them were saying you'd run away because of the Reign of Terror——"

Indignation flung off tiredness and remorse. It was a blazing Moppy that turned on Wriggles. "Did you think I couldn't face the music?" she demanded. "Pooh! I'd forgotten all about it when I went."

A cloud lifted from Wriggles's face. He had felt that if Moppy were a coward his world would rock. He was, he knew. But Moppy had always been his ideal of brave resource.

"Did you hear about the monkey, Wriggles?" questioned Moppy, indignation having loosed her tongue.

Wriggles nodded. "Wish I'd seen it," he sighed.

"How did it get there?"

" People say it was a runaway monkey."

" Like me," giggled Moppy.

" There's a circus somewhere near, and the monkey got loose. I don't think it's been caught yet."

" Mustn't it be enjoying itself!" chuckled Moppy. " I hope it's free for a very long time. Mother and Dad all right?" she asked, with would-be carelessness.

" Yes," said Wriggles briefly. He did not add that although he had not been absolutely forbidden to meet Moppy, yet Daddie had purposely given him an errand which he had hoped would make it impossible.

" The child ignored your feelings. We will ignore her existence," Daddie had decided when he had come home and heard from a very upset mummie the story of her desperate anxiety before the strange Brown Owl had telephoned.

" If you think it's the best punishment. But only for a tiny while," Mummie had agreed.

So Moppy's arrival home was very flat. There was not even the excitement of scolding and forgiveness.

" There's some supper on the table for you, and then you'd better get off to bed," Daddie said. He did not look away from the garden hose.

" And mind you have a bath. You are very grubby," added Mummie, without the hint of a greeting smile.

CHAPTER X

A Midnight Visitor

Moppy was having a disturbed night.

It may have been the hot night; it may have been the jam puffs. It may have been conscience, or it may have been all three.

She deserved the horrid dreams she got, of course.

But one was too frightening for anything.

She was dreaming that she was in the monkey house at the Zoo. No, not the monkey house, but the ape house or the gorilla house, if there was such a thing. Anyway, the one place in the world where all the biggest creatures of the monkey family were gathered together. They were screeching and gibbering and pelting her with coco-nuts, and the biggest of all seemed to be lurching towards her to seize her in its hairy arms.

It was more than any little girl could stand. She leapt away from him only to knock herself against the bars of the cage that she seemed to be sharing with the monkeys. She tore at the bars with her hands, but they would not give. How could she escape, she asked herself in terror? Luckily the bang had brought escape with it. It woke her up, and she found herself pulling at bars indeed. But they were the bars of her own bed, not of any monkeys' cage. The door that led from her room to Wriggles's was open, and a very scared Wriggles was peering in.

" Moppy! what is it?" he whispered.

" Are you having nightmare too?" began Moppy. And then she stopped petrified.

The noise was not a dream noise only. It was in the house. A peculiar shrill squealing was piercing upwards from the kitchen. Interspersed with it were the yelps and growls of Wisp.

Others besides the children were hearing it.

There was a hurried opening of doors. The children peeped out of Moppy's.

Daddie was tearing downstairs.

" Stay where you are," he was commanding Mummie, but she flew after him brandishing a poker.

The children followed. The noise might make their blood freeze, but they just had to see what it was, and anyway, they did not wish to lose sight of Mummie and Daddie.

The next moment a comforting chuckle floated up from Daddie.

" Come along as quietly as you can," he called.

On tiptoe the amazed trio reached the now open kitchen door.

A candle in the passage gave them enough light to see.

" Oh!" gasped Mummie.

" My monkey!" exclaimed Moppy.

" Don't let Wisp be hurt!" entreated Wriggles.

" Wisp is all right at present. It's worth watching for a minute," whispered Daddie.

Wisp, every hair bristling with rage and bewilderment, was engaged in heroic combat with Moppy's monkey friend of the morning.

Not that anyone would care to claim him as a friend in his present mood of hate.

Now Wisp was no mean fighter. In fact, there was not a dog for miles round of whom he stood in fear. But the monkey had weapons that Wisp had never encountered before.

The squealing worried him, as his enemy had evidently meant it should, and the monkey's cunning was superb. He was far too sensible to remain upon the floor, and, between his thrusts, he would spring now hither, now thither, in a way that completely addled Wisp's straightforward brain.

As they watched, Wisp put his forepaws on the

table and gazed half fascinated at the tiny impish face peering down at him. The monkey's eyes stood out like points of light, and they never once seemed to leave the face of the dog.

Suddenly the monkey leaped across to the dresser. Almost before the terrier could turn he was on Wisp's back, then up again on the table screeching triumphantly through a mouthful of poor Wisp's fur.

" Daddie!" cried Moppy and Wriggles.

" Time I took a hand," agreed Daddie, and snatching up a broom he advanced to battle.

Then for the first time the monkey took his eyes off Wisp.

He treated Daddie to an even more evil expression than Wisp, and, having decided that danger was threatening from another quarter, he made up his mind that further attack was useless.

He took one flying leap from the table to the top of the open window through which he had evidently entered, and disappeared into the darkness outside.

" Up the water-pipe on to the roof," guessed Daddie.

But Wisp refused to believe his enemy had departed.

The monkey had taken many flying leaps, and had reappeared more dangerous than ever. Wisp was learning from the cunning of his foe. He dashed wildly round the kitchen barking and yelping and trying some clumsy leaps of his own. He whined and he sniffed, and he headed away from all the human endearments that he usually adored.

Daddie, Mummie, Wriggles, and Moppy all joined common cause in their endeavour to soothe the outraged Wisp.

When at last, still quivering and distraught, he allowed himself to drink a little milk from Moppy's saucer, it was too late to remember that Moppy had not been forgiven.

"Never, never again shall Wisp have a window open at night. Not even if the thermometer bursts itself with heat," decreed Mummie, as she looked round her ravaged kitchen.

"So it was your monkey, was it, Moppy?" questioned Daddie, with mock severity. "I wish you'd be careful what friends you ask to the house."

"I didn't ask him, Daddie," denied Moppy, with a pitying eye on Wisp's scars.

"It's your monkey tricks that brought him, then," persisted Daddie. "Like to like, you know."

But Moppy had seen the twinkle in Daddie's eyes and knew she was forgiven.

Altogether the monkey's visit seemed to have done Moppy a good turn. It was difficult even at school to be very distant to a child who had had such an exciting midnight adventure. Miss Masters was only human. In her desire to hear of Wisp's fight she could not make too stinging a comment upon the twenty order marks that greeted her.

Besides, she understood from Miss Harris and the generous Miss Whittle that Moppy had seemed terribly sorry.

CHAPTER XI

The Circus Passes

" Your monkey's been caught, Moppy," announced Daddie, looking up from his paper a few days later at breakfast. " And his name is Lucifer."

" Poor Lucifer, I wonder if he's very sorry," said Moppy.

" Anyway, the town can have its windows open again," laughed Mummie.

Wisp's fight had actually been considered important enough to appear in the local paper together with the other misdeeds of Lucifer. Since hearing of it the more nervous inhabitants of Comfrey Hill had been careful to sleep with shut windows.

" Awful sillies, I think," had been Moppy's comment. " People might as well die of fright as of stuffiness."

" And," continued Daddie, " the circus to which he belongs is coming here to-day. It will parade the streets at noon, and Lucifer, instead of driving in his cage with his fellow monkeys—who by the way have been cutting him since his return—will be especially led on a trustworthy chain, so that everyone may see the scamp that has held them in jeopardy. Clever circus proprietor! He knows how to advertise his circus."

" Oh, Daddie, we *must* see him! Can't we leave school early?" begged Moppy.

Daddie shook his head.

" No, I'm not being unkind," he explained, as something almost like tears of disappointment glistened in Moppy's eyes. " The procession will pass by both your schools. It gives the route. I don't suppose anyone will be hard-hearted enough not to let you watch."

And so it proved.

Moppy indeed was pushed forward by her thrilled school-fellows with an " Oh, Miss Masters, you would like to see Lucifer who fought Wisp, wouldn't you?" But it really wasn't necessary. And with ecstatic giggles of delight the whole of the Junior School raced to the bottom of their beloved garden at five minutes to twelve and took up their stand on benches and on a kitchen table that a kind caretaker had provided. So well were they above the enclosing fence and shrubs, that not even the tiniest babe could help seeing. Ann, feeling that she really must meet Lucifer again in company with Moppy, had sidled away from her own First class and thrust herself in amongst the powers of the Upper Second.

Before long two Wild West bare-back outriders came galloping along to herald the nearness of the show.

The next moment it burst into vision.

" There's Lucifer. He *does* look different!" pitied Moppy and Ann together.

Poor Lucifer! As he dejectedly shambled along on all fours, chained by the side of a real black man, he certainly did look different from the knowing creature who had taken possession of the booking-office, and from the screeching malice who had vanquished Wisp.

As he passed Moppy and Ann he turned towards them a pathetic wizened face.

" You might look the other way," it seemed to plead.

Moppy and Ann squeezed hands in sympathy.

But behind Lucifer was a sight that soon drew their eyes and thoughts.

Padding along were four elephants. Their trunks were swinging from side to side in the hope of chance buns. Their small eyes were registering their disapproval of the stinginess of the empty-handed children behind the fence.

" If we'd only known!" regretted the school.

The biggest elephant turned his gaze to the other side of the road. A baker's hand-cart loaded with bread was drawn up by the pavement just in front of him. The huge creature stretched out his trunk and seized a loaf.

" Oh!" laughed the children.

" Oh, the generous darling!" they gasped the next minute. For the elephant, instead of keeping his prize for himself, had passed it on to the one just behind.

Then they clutched their neighbours' hands and watched, for the elephant was seizing another loaf. This, too, he passed behind.

He gave away a third.

Then he stretched out his trunk a fourth time to secure a loaf for himself.

But, alas, a cruel fate was to intervene.

Out of the gate opposite, with his basket on his back, came a red-faced, shouting fury of a baker. The elephant swung aside his trunk and passed on hungry.

" What a shame!" chorused the school.

" He's a *horrid* man. He's not a sport at all," declared Moppy.

Anyway, he had no sense of fun. For he stood scowling after the departing elephants, muttering vehement words about " thieving creatures ".

" The elephants were rather like us when we took

those puffs and things, weren't they, Moppy?" whispered Ann.

Moppy coloured. She had been trying hard not to think so. Those jam puffs had lain heavily on another place besides Moppy's chest. She had not felt happy about them ever since she'd come home. And thieving was such a nasty word.

" Wish we could pay that baker," she told herself for the umpteenth time.

" You could, you know," whispered an inconvenient conscience.

" Don't know who he was," demurred Moppy.

" But the Biddam Brown Owl could find out," persisted conscience.

Moppy sighed. She never had enough money, and whenever she got any nowadays she did want to lavish it on nice things for Betty. She was sure that she and Ann must have eaten quite half a crown's worth of puffs and pies and bread. And although Ann could easily have paid her share, it seemed sort of mean to ask so tiny a person to go shares. No, Moppy must be responsible for it all by herself. And she just couldn't stand this grumbling conscience any longer.

" Could you lend me two and six and a stamp, Daddie?" she asked that evening. " I'll earn the money somehow and pay you back, I pr-romise.

But I want it all at once, and not in driblets. You won't mind waiting, will you?"

" I'll wait till Christmas," smiled Daddie. He thought that Moppy's Christmas presents might be a surer source of income than her capacity for earning.

The next day Moppy invested in a postal order, and sat down to write a letter to "Mr. Baker". She sent it care of Brown Owl.

A few days later the postman brought her a letter of her very own. It was written in fine, careful writing. Moppy tore it open and devoured it. The sloping writing was quite easy to read. But its contents were far too interesting to be kept to herself.

" It's from my baker, and he must be a nice man. Do listen, everybody," she cried.

" Dear Missy,

" I have pleasure in replying to your letter of the 9th instant. All I can say is that if you and your little mate could eat two and sixpenny worth of my pastries and not be ill then you're champion, and it'll be a mighty fine advert for them. You shouldn't have bothered about the money, dear Miss, for I shouldn't have sold what was lying about. And anyway, I was insured, so didn't stand to lose. If you don't know what ' insured ' means, ask your dad. I'm glad the cookies were of use to you. My little daughter, Daphne, and you made friends that day. She is a Brownie. I gave her that two and six for herself, and she is sending it to help some poor Brownie Pack, you will like to know."

" There! isn't that lovely? Oh, I'm ever so glad I sent the postal order. Daphne was one of the two Brownies by the rushes. I must tell Ann." And Moppy flew off to school more fleet-footed than ever. The jam puffs had been changed from leaden weights to fairy messengers.

CHAPTER XII

Brownies in the Making

The Rectory garden was full of Brownies that afternoon.

It was the first few minutes of the Brownie meeting.

The Pack had danced in its Fairy Ring round Brown Owl; it had shooed away any spoilsport Boggarts that might be lurking near, so everything should have been all right. Yet Iris, dutifully inspecting her Elf Six, was not quite satisfied. Generally Brown Owl held inspection herself. Just occasionally she passed on the duty to her Sixers. Iris was always sorry when this happened.

She stopped in a worried way before a woebegone-looking recruit with an absurd plait of mouse-coloured hair.

"Where's your Brownie smile, Elsie?" she asked apologetically.

Moppy checked her own beam and heaved a tragic sigh.

" Elsie never has her Brownie smile. She's just spoiling our Six," she complained.

" I'm Sixer," quietly reminded Iris. She knew from her own experience that Moppy's candid comments could very often hurt.

" And I'm Second," smiled a red-haired stocky little Brownie in spectacles, called Bess. She was not nervous like Iris, and was happily preparing to take her place when she flew up. She loved Moppy, but she was the only Brownie in the Pack stolid enough to withstand, when necessary, the rush of Moppy's personality. From the crown of her ruddy head to the tip of her sturdy feet she just radiated reliability.

Elsie had replaced a Brownie called Leila, who had left the neighbourhood. Leila had been a black-eyed dancing little creature with keenness written all over her. She had skipped after Moppy like an attendant fairy. It really hurt Moppy to see Elsie's forlorn figure standing in the place of Leila's, and it certainly did alter the look of the Six. Moppy longed to shove Elsie in there and shove her out here, and generally to stir her up with a pin. She was thinking that she could do it better if she had official status.

" I ought to be Second," she retorted with rare temper.

Bessie smiled serenely. She quite agreed, but Brown Owl had chosen her, so that was that.

Brown Owl, seeing signs of trouble, came towards the Elf Six.

" Anything wrong?" she asked.

" I don't see how you'll ever be able to enrol Elsie, Brown Owl," exclaimed Moppy.

" Why?"

" She never has her Brownie smile."

" Are you helping her to have one?"

" It doesn't seem worth while. If she does, it's such a poor one," evaded Moppy.

" If it's Elsie's best, that's all that matters for the present. I certainly shall never be satisfied with anything but an ear-to-ear beam from Moppy, though," warned Brown Owl, as she passed on.

In spite of Brown Owl's words, Moppy could not bring herself to leave Elsie alone that afternoon. When the Sixes went into their corners to practise knots she began again.

" I can't think why you're such a little misery, Elsie," she exclaimed. " When you live in a toyshop, too! We *all* envy you."

And indeed they did. For Elsie's mother and father kept quite the nicest toyshop in the town. It was from that shop that Iris had bought the beautiful baby doll that was now dressed and sitting on Betty's bed. There was not a Brownie that did not beg to be taken down that part of the High Street where the toyshop had its home. And at Christmas snub noses were made snubbier still as they pressed against its panes in wonder at the trains passing through their tunnels, and the dolls asleep in their cradles or muffled up in winter coats and bonnets.

" I can't *have* the toys," dully objected Elsie.

" But you can look at them and make up stories about them," cried Moppy, wriggling her impatience at such lost opportunities.

At the magic word " stories " the Six grew alert. For Moppy's powers of story-telling were very famed.

" Do tell us a story, Moppy," it clamoured.

" Don't suppose there's time."

" Begin one, then," begged a dimpled Brownie called Tilda.

Moppy looked at Tilda, and turned afresh to reproach poor Elsie. If Elsie was envied as a toyshop girl, Tilda's home came next in the ambitions of most small Brownies. For Tilda lived in a sweetshop. She was rather like a particularly round pink pear-drop herself, when the white sugar was all fresh on it, of course, not when it had been long in a sticky bag. She was all beams and chub.

" Look how different Tilda is." exclaimed Moppy.

" She can't eat all the chocolates and sweets, but it jolly well doesn't make her look a dismal Jennie."

" Oh, never mind Tilda and Elsie, let's have the story!" cried Iris, the peacemaker. " We can tie our knots while we listen."

" Very well," conceded Moppy. " Sit on me, Ann. I want to tie my string round your wrist. You can make your knot round the rung of the chair." She looked round the garden, and her glance fell upon a clump of poppies. " I'll tell you a story about the Pinkpopperies," she decided.

" Mrs. Pinkpopperie and her family had been having great sorrows. First, Mr. Pinkpopperie died, and then little Rollypole would not grow into a nice flower. Spinneyspice, the little open bud, thought he would stay as he was, and his poor old mother was so anxious about him.

" One day Mrs. Pinkpopperie went to see a very old friend of hers (her name was Mrs. Tuliplop), and she had a little boy.

" Mrs. Pinkpopperie and Mrs. Tuliplop decided to send their children to Mr. Pepperpot's school.

" When the little boys heard that they were going to school they were very excited. The next morning they went off to Mr. Pepperpot's, and the boys were rather frightened.

4

" Mr. Pepperpot had on yellow silk trousers, and a little tiny short blue satin coat, pink fur boots, and a green wrapper about his shoulders.

" He was a short and thin little man, but even Mrs. Pinkpopperie and Mrs. Tuliplop were rather afraid of him. They left their boys at the school and returned home very dismal."

" Tu-whit—tu-whit, tu-whit whit whit!" came Brown Owl's signal.

" *To be continued*," chanted Moppy, jumping up.

" Oh!" sadly accepted the Six. It knew it had heard the last of the Pinkpopperies and was sorry about it. For, although Moppy was the staunchest of persons to her real flesh and blood friends, yet she had a way of dropping the friends of her imagination when a fresh fancy came into her mind.

" We're going to play the Germ Game," announced Brown Owl.

" How *lovely!*" chorused the Pack.

" How do you play it? How do you play it?" feverishly demanded Elsie of her neighbours. It had not been played since she had joined the Pack. Most of the Pack were too busy squealing out their excitement and shamelessly begging to be one of the four Boggarts to pay any attention to Elsie's ineffective demands.

Moppy, however, thirsting to educate this recruit, and perhaps a little remorseful of her former rough treatment, stopped her jumping ecstasies to fling a few words of explanation.

" Four of us are Boggarts, Germ Boggarts this time, not Temper Boggarts. One's the germ that gets into dirty nails, another the Boggart that gets into dirty teeth. Another gets into your mouth if it can, and another gets into your hair. They hide and rush out at us while we dance around. If one of them catches a Brownie she has to remember which germ it is. If she wants to escape from the Boggart she has to do the action that wards off the germ—brush her teeth, breathe through her nose and all that, see? She has to do it before the germ can count ten, too. If she can't, she's dead."

" Who wins?" shrilled Elsie. " Who wins? The germ who catches the most Brownies?"

" *No!*" cried a shocked Moppy. " We never allow a germ to win in *our* Pack. It's a Six that wins; the Six that loses the least Brownies. The germ may catch some Brownies—I 'spect it'll catch you—but we diddle it in the end!"

Most of the Brownies were good at running about, but Moppy was best of all. By the time the meeting was over there should have been very little breath left in her body, but she managed to find enough to dash off to Betty Horpe's cottage to put in ten minutes there before returning home.

" Thought you'd like to know what the Pack's been doing this afternoon," she cried, as she flung herself in. " Oh, Betty, won't it be scrum-scrum-scrummy when you can come yourself?"

" Yes," agreed Betty.

" We've been doing knots and signalling and the Germ Game. That's to help us know our health rules. We often play games that help us with our tests. There're awfully jolly games about the Union Jack, too.

" How clever I shall be when I know all those things!" exclaimed Betty.

" *Clever!*" scorned Moppy. " A Brownie doesn't learn things to be clever. She learns them so that she can be useful to other people."

Mother and Daddie and Brown Owl might have smiled a rueful little smile had they heard this remark of Moppy's. But Moppy saw nothing funny about it. She always meant to be useful and a really truly Brownie, only each day came tumbling along crowded with things that pulled you this way and that, and sometimes the Brownie part of her got pushed on one side without her even knowing it.

" Some of our tests, like throwing a ball and hopping round a figure of eight, seem just fun for ourselves," continued Moppy. " But Brown Owl explained to us once that the stronger and fitter we are the more use we can be to other people, and it makes our Brownie smile awfully easy, too, when we feel bubbly and well. Then after you're enrolled you must try to become a Golden Bar Brownie."

" Whatever's that?" cried Betty.

" Well, some Packs say Second Class Brownie, but we don't. We think a Golden Bar Brownie sounds much more magical. You see, it's like this. When a Brownie can do certain things, she's standing firm on the Golden Ground with her hands stretched out ready to help. At least, that's sort of how Brown Owl put it when she gave me my Golden Bar. Look! I've got it on here above my left pocket."

Betty gazed admiringly at her pattern Brownie.

" Then when we can do lots of other things still, like remembering messages and bandaging fingers, and cooking rice puddings and making cups of tea, then we're Golden Hand Brownies. First Class Brownies the dull people say. You wear your Golden Hand just *above* your Golden Bar. Iris is the only Brownie in our Pack who has one. You must notice next time she comes and sees you in uniform. I shall have mine very soon. I should have had it long ago if it hadn't been for the Nature Study Test."

Poor Moppy! This was the one test that kept standing obstinately in her path. She had been trying to pass it ever since last autumn. To plant something and watch it grow seemed to require just a little more patience than Moppy possessed.

She had gaily started off with an acorn. It was such a nice satisfactory thing that could begin its life in water. Such a ducky little green glass held it, too. So small that it could go beautifully on Moppy's bedroom mantelpiece. " It'll be jolly to watch it sprouting both underneath and on top," she had decided.

But a day soon came when she spilt the water in one of her headlong rushes.

" I haven't time to fill up now, but I'll give you a lovely clean lake before bedtime," she promised the acorn as she replaced it in the empty glass.

But several bedtimes passed before she remembered, and the poor sprouting roots shrivelled.

Then she turned helter-skelter to bulbs. She planted pheasant-eyed narcissi in a pot and took them down into the cellar. But, thanks to the ill-fated acorn, she was late in starting, and the pot was not ready to come up with Mother's bowls. Christmas excitements began for Moppy even before December. How could she remember to keep her bulbs damp in the midst of parties and presents and Christmas good turns? By the time humdrum life began again the fibre was dry as sawdust, and the bulbs were ruined.

With the spring came the planting of seeds, but either Wisp gardened with her and scratched them up, or no obliging rain pretended to be her watering-can, so nothing worth showing Brown Owl ever grew.

There was mustard and cress, certainly, but that was so easy to grow that Moppy had disdained to count it.

All her hopes were now centred on a late sowing of lettuces. But there were prickings to be done, and a warfare to be waged with slugs and snails before ever the perfect lettuce could evolve. So Moppy felt a little shaky.

" I shall have my Golden Hand very soon," she repeated just to encourage herself. " Isn't it a lovely thing to have?"

" It *is*," agreed Betty.

She spread out her own little thin hands and thought about it long after Moppy had left. Supposing they were golden! Supposing they shone and glimmered in that little cottage! It seemed too much of a fairy story ever to be true.

Brown Owl found her looking at them when she

came in half an hour later to pay her Post Brownie a
surprise visit.

" Penny for your thoughts, Betty," she challenged.

Betty flushed.

" I—I was thinking I could be a Golden Hand
Brownie," she whispered. " Wasn't it silly, when I'm
a Post Brownie and only a recruit?"

" Not a scrap silly," comforted Brown Owl. " It's
never too early to start along the road. Post Brown
Owl has been writing and telling me about some of
her other Post Brownies. She says one of her Golden
Hand Brownies is a little girl who always has to lie
flat on her back. She passed her Signalling Test like
that, and the Scoutmaster who came to examine her
really couldn't find anything wrong for which to take
off a mark. She made her fire—you have to do that,
you know, before you can get your Golden Hand—
in an iron tray on a wooden board put over her bed.
Don't you think that was splendid?"

Betty's big blue eyes showed that she did.

" And I think the goldenest part of it all was how
she just wouldn't let her ill health be a hindrance. It
must have made her mother awfully happy, mustn't
it?"

Betty nodded.

" How can I begin?" she asked.

" I should begin by helping Mother."

" I'm going to get up soon, you know," confided Betty. " I must ask Mummie what I can do."

But when Betty asked, Mrs. Horpe was rather like a wet blanket. She could never get out of her mind the days when Betty had been so desperately ill with rheumatic fever.

" Silly child, of course you can't lift saucepans and sweep rooms. If you're going to try that sort of thing when my back's turned, and make yourself ill again, I shall wish you weren't a Brownie, that I shall."

Betty sighed. Ever so far off, the Golden Hand was beckoning. She did so want to follow.

" I won't, truly I won't, Mums," she promised. " But there must be something I can do. Couldn't I iron for you sitting down?"

Mrs. Horpe sniffed at the idea.

" A pernickety job like ironing! Why, it takes all my wits and more to get it to the ladies' liking. Sleeves and tucks and what not! Listen to her!"

" But the hankies, Mummie," pleaded Betty. " Course I could iron them; now, couldn't I?"

Mrs. Horpe hesitated. There were no fal-lals about handkerchiefs certainly, and if it made the child happy——

" Well, we'll see," she promised.

CHAPTER XIII

The Week-end Camp

" Oh! Moppy, you are cross this afternoon," sighed Iris.

It was the beginning of the half-term holiday, and Moppy was spending it with Iris and Ann. It was further on in June than ever before, for Easter had been at its latest, and had made the term a very short one. The weather was lovely, but none of the three were enjoying it very much, not even Ann, for Moppy had once more lost her Brownie smile, and again it was all through Wriggles.

For the Wolf Cubs were having a week-end camp. The Cubmaster had sprung it on them as a surprise at last Pack meeting. All the Comfrey Hill schools were having the same half-term, so most of the Cubs were available, and the Cubmaster had stolen a day from his summer holiday so as to have Monday free himself.

" Greedies," Moppy had declared. " Isn't the August camp enough for them?"

She had been so glum about it that Mummie had said "Thank you very much" directly Mrs. Pritchard had asked her little daughter to stay. She had packed Moppy off to Iris and Ann quite early on this Friday afternoon, so that her gloomy face should not spoil Wriggles's pleasure.

But that did not make things very much better, for the Pritchards' orchard stretched right down to the meadow where the Wolf Cubs were going to camp the next morning. The orchard was a very favourite spot for Iris and Ann to play in. Some of the gnarled fruit-trees were so cosy and quaint that they loved to bring them into their games. The grass grew high between them, and was blue with forget-me-nots. It made a lovely fairyland.

They took Moppy down there without thinking. But instead of playing, Moppy gazed over the hedge and pictured the tents that the Cubmaster would be putting up that night in readiness for his Pack.

The thought of it made poor Moppy green with envy.

"Iris," she suddenly exclaimed, "you've got a bell tent in the loft, haven't you? I noticed it once when we were playing hide-and-seek. Mayn't we have a week-end camp of our own out here? It'll be practice for us when we're at Urchin Bay."

Iris shook her head. " I'm sure Mummie'll never let us camp out by ourselves," she declared. " I told her what you said about Urchin Bay. She's awfully pleased for you to stay with us there, but we mayn't camp."

Moppy pouted. " If we mayn't camp there, I won't——" she began. Then she remembered that Betty was coming to Urchin Bay. It had been duckie of the Pritchards to ask her. They had taken on Mr. Horpe as an odd outdoor man, too, in the place of one whom they were just pensioning off. It was making an enormous difference to this family so long crippled by unemployment. Altogether the Pritchards had been bricks. She couldn't be so silly as to expect everything to turn out just as she wished. Moppy was philosopher enough to know that, even in a black monkey mood.

Well, she had no doubt that once at Urchin Bay they could find adventures enough to make those stupid little Wolf Cubs sit up, tent or no tent. No, she would not quarrel with her summer holiday, but have that tent out here in the orchard she would, Iris or no Iris.

" Mrs. Pritchard wouldn't mind you using the tent in the daytime, would she, Iris? Do ask her," she coaxed.

" If Horpe has time to put it up this afternoon you

can play in it to-morrow. But it wants several hours of sunshine on it before you can. It must be terribly damp," was Mrs. Pritchard's answer.

Had Horpe time? Of course he had. He would have found time to fetch the moon from the sky if Moppy had asked him. Under her directions he at once put up the tent at the bottom of the orchard on a spot where only a hedge divided it from to-morrow's camp.

The next morning, directly after breakfast, Mr. Pritchard drove the children with him to a neighbouring farm. Moppy went like a martyr. Generally she would have loved the geese and calves and piglets. To-day she grudged every moment that kept her from tent life.

It was well after twelve when they got back. Moppy scurried upstairs and tore the sheets and blankets off her bed.

" What *are* you doing, Moppy?" cried Iris and Ann, when they reached the room a moment later.

Moppy chuckled and threw back her curls. " *I'm* going to camp properly," she told them. " Mummie won't mind, I'm sure. The boys'll be just over the hedge, and I'll fetch Wisp this afternoon to keep me company to-night."

Iris grew red. She hummed a nervous little tune,

turned her back on Moppy, and walked to the window.

Mrs. Pritchard was out for the day, and Nannie was having a sewing day. It was quite possible for Moppy to make her preparations unnoticed. Iris didn't want to be a tell-tale, yet she was sure Moppy shouldn't be allowed to camp alone. What ought she to do about it? Anyway, she wouldn't help Moppy make up her bed. Ann wanted to, though.

" Stay here, Ann!" she called as the two were running out of the room.

Ann looked back and saw Iris's solemn face. For the moment she stayed.

Moppy, perfectly happy and intent, flew down to the kitchen. She wheedled from Cook—bacon, potatoes, a frying-pan, and all necessary oddments, and went off well laden to furnish the tent and cook her midday meal.

As she turned into the orchard she could see the smoke from the Wolf Cub camp curling up between the fruit-trees. They had made their kitchen fire close to the orchard hedge. Then their white tents came in view, and their Union Jack waving proudly aloft. Next she caught sight of the Cubs themselves. Their sleeves were rolled up and their orange scarves were glinting in the sun. They were dashing hither and thither as busy as bees.

' I'm sorry for the dinner if Wriggles is helping to cook it," she told herself.

Then she heard footsteps scrambling through the long grass.

" Moppy," cried a voice behind her.

She turned round and faced a breathless Ann.

" Moppy, I must camp with you," cried Ann. " Do let me help you fry the bacon. And here are some eggs from Biddy, my own dear hen."

Moppy beamed. She did not really like being alone. Things were much nicer when you shared them with other people, and there was generally something to talk about that just wouldn't wait. So Moppy conveniently forgot to ask whether Nannie knew, and bore off Ann with her to the tent.

The flaps were well back, for Horpe had declared that the tent was musty. " If you shut it up it'll smell shocking," he had told Moppy.

" It's just as nice a tent as any of those silly Wolf Cubs'. Aren't they little ninnies?" scoffed Moppy. " Did you know that their Cubmaster had their tents waxed and ironed, so that they would be quite certain to keep out the wet? *Oh*, I've carried these things far enough!" she cried, flinging her armful before her on to the floor of the tent. Then suddenly a tone of amazement crept into her voice.

" Ann!" she cried. " Quick! Come and look!"

She pointed in silence to the apex of the tent.

Then she and Ann stood staring upwards in a mixture of alarm and curiosity.

Hanging from the apex, like an elongated football, were thousands of motionless bees.

Ann gazed at the cluster open mouthed.

" W-what is it?" she gasped.

" It's bees swarming," Moppy whispered. " Come right in and look."

" Won't they sting?" asked Ann, shrinking back.

" Course not," reassured Moppy. " They're frightfully good tempered when they're swarming. Canon Chesney says so. He keeps bees, you know. We're awful chums, and he's told me lots about them. When they're swarming they're chock-full of honey. He says they're like old gentlemen having a nap after a very good dinner. You can ladle them into a hive with a spoon. He doesn't even wear a veil when he's taking a swarm."

She gripped Ann's hand and darted forward to get a nearer view.

As she did so her foot caught against the frying-pan that she had flung carelessly in front of her. She stumbled, pulled Ann along with her, and jerked the two of them against the pole.

The shock disturbed the hanging bees, a moment before so safely content. Several were shaken down towards the children.

Alas for Moppy's boasting! Canon Chesney's immunity was not to be hers. Even the sweetest tempered old gentleman would become testy were he awakened suddenly by a prance upon his gouty toe. Even the best tempered of bees could only regard with aversion the thickness of Moppy's hair. It was this that they flew against, and the curls refused to release their wings. Terrified by the trap, the bees used their stings.

Frightened by the sharp stabbing on forehead and face, Moppy rushed from the tent. She was followed by a screaming Ann. But no matter where they went some half-dozen bees flew around them buzzing with anger.

" Oh! Oh!" screamed Ann, dancing with a wounded leg.

CHAPTER XIV

Moppy's Swarm

Meanwhile the Cubs were having a rollicking time.

Their Cubmaster was a tall well-set-up Rover who gave so much of himself to the Pack that the cubbiest of spirits prevailed within it. At present the Cubs were admiring his efforts to make a successful suet pudding. Puddings were not his strongest point, and so watery was it that it refused to do anything but spread itself out over the cloth.

" Let's make pancakes of it, Akela," piped out a brilliant but diminutive Cub.

" And eat them with jam," hinted the fattest.

It was at this point that the screams of Ann floated over the hedge.

The Pack grew alert. " What's up?" it chorused.

It peered into the orchard.

Two little girls seemed to be prancing about with the queerest antics.

" Hulloa!" discovered Wriggles. " It's Moppy and Ann."

The orchard gate was close to them. He darted through it. The Cubmaster came too.

"It's bees," called back Akela to his Cubs. "Put some water on the fire to make it smoke, and fan the smoke this way."

He picked up Ann and ran with her towards the fire. He was followed by a distracted Moppy, vainly trying to shake the bees from her face.

The Wolf Cubs, fanning the fire with their blankets, directed its smoke towards the children.

Gradually the bees dropped stupefied away. They left two frightened little girls blinking in the smoke.

"There's a swarm on the tent pole," announced Moppy. The stings were becoming more painful, but they did not prevent her feeling important.

"Business first. Pow-wow later," decreed the Cubmaster. "I must squash the ones in your hair."

The idea was displeasing to Moppy, to Ann, and to most of the Pack. He then approached Moppy with a pointed knife in his hand. Moppy tried to leave off blinking. Her cheek was gaily swelling. It was difficult to smile. But Ann's leg was swelling too. She must set a standard of bravery.

"Just get your stings out, old lady," explained the Cubmaster. "We'll begin on you to show the little one that she needn't be frightened."

Wriggles, with a cut onion in readiness to clap upon the swellings, looked on, paler than ever. He was torn between faith in Akela and fear for Moppy.

Other Wolf Cubs, more impersonally interested, had wandered through the gate towards the tent.

"The swarm's still there," they came back to report.

"Whose swarm is it?" one of them asked.

"I expect nobody'll ever know," said Akela. "It's evidently a swarm from a distance."

In spite of stings and swellings Moppy became alert.

"I know a rhyme about bees," she cried. "Canon Chesney told it me.

> ' A swarm in May
>   Is worth a load of hay,
>   A swarm in June
>   Is worth a silver spoon,
>   A swarm in July
>   Isn't worth a butterfly.' "

"That's right," laughed Akela.

"This swarm's worth a silver spoon then," she announced. "And I found it, didn't I?"

"You certainly did," grinned Akela. "And the swarm found you."

"Mightn't I have it?" persisted Moppy.

"I suppose you might. But it's not of much use

to you in that tent, is it? A swarm of bees isn't like a pet dog, you know."

" I can sell it," announced Moppy.

" Mercenary Mary!" exclaimed Akela.

There were times when Moppy chose to ignore words that she did not understand.

" Can't I sell it?" she persisted.

" Tent pole and all?" teased Akela.

But here Wriggles, also a friend of Canon Chesney's, rushed into the gap.

" We'll take the swarm," he stammered.

" Where's your skep?" laughed Akela.

Wriggles was so eager to second Moppy and to offer consolation for her unsightly stings that his mind began to seethe with ingenious suggestions.

" We'll t-take it in a pail," he cried, and snatched up one that stood by the fire. " And c-can't we have a cloth or something?"

" There's a sheet in the tent," chipped in Moppy.

" Shouldn't be," reproved the Senior Sixer.

" We can wrap the pail in it, then," exclaimed Wriggles.

" And Canon Chesney can buy it and put it in a hive," settled Moppy.

Akela, seeing that there was more in their plan than

scatter-brained nonsense, decided to take the matter seriously, and to direct the brain waves of Wriggles along the right channels. His long arm easily held the pail close enough beneath the cluster of bees to catch them after they had been dislodged by a sharp shake. Luck was with them. The queen bee must happily have entered the pail early, and all the others obediently followed.

It was not long before Canon Chesney, summoned by two jubilant and excited Wolf Cubs, appeared on the scene with a straw skep.

The Pack gleefully showed him a shrouded pail.

" Why didn't you wait for me?" he queried.

Akela laughed, and tweaked Wriggles' ear. " I was tender-hearted, sir, and wouldn't quench this chap's ingenuity," he confessed.

" What's the price of a silver spoon, Canon Chesney?" grimly demanded a mump-like Moppy.

" It varies greatly, my child," smiled the Canon. " But there's another saying I haven't taught you. It's unlucky not to give gold for a swarm."

He fumbled in his pocket for a pound note. " A poor thing, but to-day's equivalent for gold," he deprecated, and held it out to Moppy.

In spite of stiffness and pain Moppy managed a grateful smile.

Then she caught the reproachful glances of many Wolf Cubs.

" If it hadn't been for us, she'd still have been running away from those bees, wouldn't she, Akela?" hinted Wriggles' Sixer.

Moppy flushed, and braced herself to renounce. It was so, and fair was fair with Moppy.

" I'll share it, if you like," she offered. " But I did want it to buy a uniform for our Post Brownie. Post Brownies needn't have uniforms, of course. But it's so much more lovely and real if they do. And I did want Betty's to be a present from me. She could buy it herself gradually, but it's one of my dreams to give it her. If there was all that money I could get her nice brown shoes and stockings too. And I did want just one half - crown for myself," she added wistfully. " It's to pay off a very private debt."

Akela smiled. He had heard about the Post Brownie from Wriggles, who had anxiously inquired whether there were Post Wolf Cubs too. It had been a blow to Wriggles to learn that there were none as yet.

" I'll explain to these chaps, and I'm sure they'll understand," he smiled. " And if ever we have a Post Wolf Cub you'll try and help us, won't you?"

" *Rather!*" agreed Moppy.

The Wolf Cubs had been anything but silly ninnies;

in fact, they had proved themselves a good deal more sensible than Moppy. Wriggles with his suggestions and his cut onion had been bright and useful.

It was all rather hurtful to Moppy's conceit.

Then there was poor little Ann limping along so bravely with wet tobacco bandaged round her chubby leg.

Certainly she didn't look as ugly as Moppy. But her sting was hurting badly, Moppy knew. And all that angry buzzing had been very frightening for her.

Again Moppy felt terribly ashamed at having led Ann into trouble. That pound note too. Moppy had talked so glibly of it being hers. But wasn't it just as much Ann's? Ann had shared only too unfortunately in the startling discovery.

Moppy tucked Ann's hand under her arm and spoke.

" Ann," she said in a very small voice, " it's—it's your pound just as much as mine. I can't think why I didn't see that earlier. What would you like to do with your half?"

Ann turned her smutty, tear-stained face trustfully up to Moppy.

" Course I want just what you said," she cried. " You to give Betty her uniform."

" Not *me*. You and me, then," corrected a grateful Moppy.

" I've a better idea still," she cried the next moment. " Let's not even say it's from you and me, but just call it from the Elf Six. I think that would be nicer still, don't you?"

" Oh, *yes*," agreed Ann.

But though Ann was perfectly content with Moppy's generalship, Nannie had a great deal to say when the wounded warriors presented themselves before her. " I'll thank you to get into trouble by yourself next time," she had ended up. " But that's a thing you never can do, I'm thinking. And as for that tent, Horpe shall take it down and put it away this very afternoon. There shall be no burning of frying-pans and fingers and worse *this* half-term holiday." Which was a hard saying, but an ease to Iris's problem. Moppy would certainly sleep in her bedroom that night.

Quietly Iris helped Moppy return the contents of the tent to their rightful quarters. She was dreadfully sorry for Moppy.

But Moppy's face had become too stiff and swollen for her really to mind.

CHAPTER XV

In the Balance

The next Tuesday was not the happiest of days for Moppy. The bees' stings had given her the funniest tilt to mouth and nose.

" Toothache, Moppy?" inquired her pitying school-fellows.

Had she not boasted to Ann of her knowledge it might have been quite exciting to have explained that she had tumbled into a swarm of bees. But, on think-ing it over, her dash from the tent had seemed such a humiliating sequel and the speedy vanishing of the tent seemed more so.

Then Tuesday afternoon was Pack meeting, and it had all to be gone over again with those Brownies who were not school-fellows as well.

Upon Eisie the sight of Moppy had the queerest effect.

At the first glance her usual down-at-the-mouth expression changed into the broadest smile.

" He!" she suddenly emitted. " He! He-he!!
He-he-he-he-*hee!!!*"

It was the funniest ripple of squeaks.

Moppy and the other Brownies gazed in wonder at
this usually care-worn recruit.

She was laughing, laughing uproariously.

" What's up?" demanded Moppy.

" He! He-he-he-*hee!!*" she went on giggling. " You
d-do look so comic."

The Brownies gasped. She was laughing at Moppy.
Poor wounded Moppy.

Under their reproachful gaze Elsie made frantic
efforts at control. She at last subdued her laughter to
a convulsive grin.

Brown Owl noticed the grin. She came up very
pleased.

" Well done, Elsie," she approved. " At last
you've produced a perfectly satisfactory Brownie
smile."

Then she glanced at Moppy's solemn face.

" Hulloa! Can't all the Elf Six wear its smile together?" she questioned.

" I just don't approve of Elsie's smile," pronounced
Moppy with dignity. " I don't call it a Brownie smile
when it's a smile at someone else's misfortunes."

A dimple peeped out of Brown Owl's cheek. Beneath the crowd of disapproving eyes it popped back again very quickly.

"Anyway, it may teach Elsie how wide a Brownie smile can be," consoled Brown Owl. "Catch it and keep it, Elsie, and use it in a better purpose. Then perhaps Moppy will forgive you. Will you, Moppy?"

Moppy gave as much of a smile as her one-sided face would allow.

"Yes, Brown Owl," she promised.

The Pack ended its meeting with Dodge Ball. It was a game it loved. Each Six took its turn in the middle of a ring made by the other Brownies.

The Brownies who formed the ring threw a net ball at the Brownies within. If it hit a Brownie below the knee she was out. There was much scuttling and leaping to avoid being hit, and great competition to see which Brownie could escape the longest.

The Elves went into the ring last. Presently all were hit except Moppy and Iris.

"You won't hit Moppy, will you?" cried an excited Brownie to the holder of the ball.

"No, don't hit Moppy," echoed another. "Hit Iris, won't you?"

Brown Owl overheard and looked grave. She did not think these speeches Brownie-like.

With such decided barracking it was not surprising

that, in spite of skilful leaping, Iris should soon be hit out.

A conquering Moppy was swallowed up in a crowd of admirers.

" I am glad you've won, Moppy dear," cried Tilda. " I kept telling everyone not to hit you."

" Didn't you think I was clever enough to win on my own, then?" retorted Moppy.

Tawny Owl laughed. She was very young, and did not have to be as responsible as Brown Owl. She regarded Moppy and her doings as a huge joke. Like the Pack she had hoped Moppy would win.

" Of course Iris has her Golden Hand, but she hasn't half the kudos Moppy has with the Pack, has she?" she commented to Brown Owl. " We shan't have a First Class Brownie when Iris flies up, shall we? Oh yes," she remembered, " Moppy has only one more test to pass. My word, won't the Pack revel in their Grand Howl when Moppy gains her Golden Hand?"

But Brown Owl did not answer. She took her Brownies very seriously, and was not at all sure whether Moppy was ready to be a Golden Hand Brownie.

Moppy herself had no such doubts. In fact, her thoughts just now were very full of her Golden Hand.

For Brown Owl had that day talked to the Pack about Iris flying up to the Guides. It had even been settled which Patrol Iris was to go into. She was to belong to the Robins, and her Patrol Leader would be a girl called Cicely Merryweather. The Pack thought Iris was very lucky, for Cicely's younger sister, Madge, was the Guide who was their Pack Leader. If Cicely were anything like Madge, and rumour said she was even nicer, Iris would love her patrol. She was to fly up at the end of July just before the summer holidays.

In the ordinary way the fly up would have been after the break, not before it, but, much to the sorrow of the Pack, Brown Owl was going abroad in September for some weeks, and was wishful to speed on her Brownie before she went. Although Tawny Owl could carry on with the Pack while she was away, only Brown Owl could give Iris her wings.

" P'raps Brown Owl'll give me my Golden Hand at the same time. I can pass my Nature Study Test any day now," Moppy told herself triumphantly. Fenced around by wire netting from the hoeing and raking of Wisp, fortified by soot and ministered to with orange peel and cut potato, one lettuce had not only survived all the mischances of life, but had obligingly become great and shapely in stature.

Moppy was walking home, as she often did, with

Iris and Ann, when she made a startling discovery.
" Iris!" she exclaimed, " you'll be a Guide when the
Company goes to camp. Will you go to camp with
them instead of to Urchin Bay with us?"

Iris shook her head. " Course not. I'll still be much
more of a Brownie than a Guide."

Moppy looked relieved. She had been ready to con-
gratulate, but it was very nice to feel that she would
not have to see both Wriggles and Iris depart with
camping kit.

" That's rather jolly," she decided. " Then you
and I will have our first time camp together. For I'll
be a Guide too by next summer. I expect I'll fly up
after Easter, don't they?"

" Only Golden Hand Brownies fly up though, don't
they?" said Ann.

" Of course, but I shall be one almost directly. Very
likely I'll get my Golden Hand when Iris flies up."

The two little sisters glanced uneasily at each other.

" What's the matter?" demanded Moppy.

Iris grew red. " Nothing," she stammered.

Moppy looked at them curiously.

" There is something," she retorted. " Tell me."

Iris's chin took an obstinate jut. Gentle though she
was, Moppy knew it was sometimes quite impossible
to move her. She turned to Ann.

" Tell me, Ann," she coaxed.

" Iris thinks——" began Ann miserably.

" Be quiet, Ann," cried Iris.

" Go on, Ann," said Moppy.

Ann never disobeyed Moppy, so she did.

" Iris is so afraid Brown Owl mayn't give you your Golden Hand," she faltered.

Moppy stopped dead and looked at the two in horror.

" Why ever not!" she demanded. " I can cook a most beautiful rice pudding. Daddie had two helps of it. And I can get stains off the knives quicker than anybody. And I often clean the silver for Mummie. And when Wriggles cut his finger the other day, I bound it up most beautifully."

" I know, Moppy," humbly agreed Iris. " I expect I'm quite wrong, only, you see, Brown Owl does think such a lot of character."

" What's wrong with my character?" asked an amazed Moppy.

Ann looked on, not understanding.

She knew that as Elves she and Iris and Moppy should go about helping others, not themselves. She always tried to remember that, even when she wasn't singing it at a Pack meeting. She particularly remembered when there were strawberries for tea, and she had the dish before other people. She knew that the Gnomes should make a speciality of helping Mother in their homes, and that the Pixies should be keen on helping people who are in fixes. She knew, too, that if you tried your very best to remember and do such things, then you were a really truly Brownie; while if you only joined a Brownie Pack for the fun of it and never thought of yourself as a Brownie except at Pack meetings and picnics, then you were a rotten Brownie who bore a remarkable likeness to a Boggart.

But as for all this having anything to do with a long dull word like character—well, Ann just shook her head over it. Moppy and Iris, both being in double figures and pretty bright for that, did understand.

"What's wrong with my character?" repeated Moppy.

"Nothing," stammered Iris. She was seeming terribly priggish, she knew, but she didn't mean to be. She would hate Moppy not to have her Golden Hand. It was because she had wanted her to have it so much that she had been silly enough to chatter to Ann about this terrible possibility.

"You're a darling, Moppy," she cried impulsively. "But—but, well for one thing, you don't always obey, do you? And Brown Owl always makes so much of that part of the Brownie Law."

5

" I obey when I think about it," muttered Moppy. Then she suddenly swung away. Tears were swelling up in her eyes.

" I think you're both just horrid and ridiculous," she cried, clenching her hands.

And she clenched them all the more because a little voice inside her was now treacherously agreeing with all that Iris was saying.

Brownies on whose hands the gold was beginning to glimmer didn't establish Reigns of Terror. They didn't carry off smaller Brownies unbeknown to their worrying mothers. They didn't——

" Oh, shut up!" Moppy told that little voice, and flew off home with her worries.

Brown Owl was also taking her worries home. The thought of denying Moppy her Golden Hand was a horrible one. But, as Iris guessed, duty was very strong with Brown Owl. Would it be good for the Pack to let a harum-scarum like Moppy gain her Golden Hand? And would it be good for this harum-scarum herself?

To one of Brown Owl's thoroughness the answer took a lot of finding

Canon Chesney thought his daughter very silent as she sat at supper with him that evening.

" Anything wrong, Robert?" he asked, creasing his eyes in their kindliest smile.

Brown Owl's name was Roberta. He had called her Robert ever since the time when, left without her mother as a schoolgirl of fifteen, she had set herself the task of caring for her father and his slum parish.

" You're as plucky as a boy," he had tenderly told her.

" Anything wrong, Robert?" he repeated.

" It's Moppy," sighed Brown Owl. " I'm wondering if I ought to be perfectly horrid."

Canon Chesney listened to the problem. But his smile was never far away as he did so. He had a very soft corner in his heart for Moppy.

" There's nothing really wrong with Moppy, Robert," he pronounced. " She'll be a fine personality when she's older. The poet Browning has so many lines that remind me of Moppy.

' All instincts immature,
All purposes unsure.

' Thoughts hardly to be packed
Into a narrow act.'

Doesn't that bring Moppy to you? Moppy with her limitless range of activities. Seemingly disobedient and irresponsible because the next moment beckons with its infinite possibilities. She'll gain her balance in time, never fear. Aren't her generous impulses already working for good? What about Betty Horpe? Would that child ever have worn the ecstatic beam she's wearing to-day if ten-year-old Moppy had not tried to tackle the problem of reconciling a disgruntled man to the universe?"

" But she always seems to be dragging other children into trouble with her," sighed Brown Owl.

" Have a private talk with her then. Tell her she's a born leader. She knows it already, so it won't do any harm. Tell her what a responsibility lies with those who are. And here's one more scrap from Browning to comfort you:

> ' Youth
> Should strive through acts uncouth
> Toward making.' "

" Perhaps," smiled Brown Owl. " But it's a shame that everybody should like her better than Iris."

Canon Chesney gravely agreed.

" It is," he admitted. " Iris is as good as gold, but that's the way of things. No one, not even the cleverest Brown Owl in the world, can direct the course of popularity. And that's not Moppy's fault, is it? She doesn't try to undermine Iris with the Pack?"

" Of course she doesn't. But I do think she thinks they're perfectly right to like her best."

Moppy has superb confidence in herself," laughed Canon Chesney.

Before next Pack meeting Moppy received a little note from Brown Owl asking her to come round.

This time Moppy did not fling herself in at the Rectory gate. The remarks of Iris and Ann were still lingering in her mind, and she was actually feeling a little shy.

Brown Owl's first words seemed reassuring.

" What about that lettuce?" she asked with a smile, for the Pack was kept well posted up in the progress of the famous lettuce.

Moppy allowed herself a chastened beam.

" Splendid," she pronounced. " I was going to tell you, Brown Owl, on Tuesday. I'm sure I can pass my Nature Test with it. It—it's the only thing I haven't done for my Golden Hand, isn't it?" she hazarded.

" Is it?" thoughtfully asked Brown Owl. " I know you're the sort of little person who likes to aim high. You wouldn't wish to think of the Golden Hand except as something very fine, would you?"

" No!" faltered Moppy.

" Then do you honestly think you come up to the standard of a Golden Hand Brownie?"

" Oh, Brown Owl, *don't*," cried Moppy. Put like that she knew she fell very far short.

" I was sure you wouldn't really think so," said Brown Owl gently. " But it's better to aim high and miss, isn't it, Moppy?"

" Then mayn't I have my Golden Hand?" cried poor Moppy.

Brown Owl was silent for a moment, then she spoke very slowly:

" This was one of the questions I asked Iris when I gave her her Golden Hand, ' Now that you know what is expected of a Golden Hand Brownie, will you do your best to carry it out?' Do you remember the answer to that?"

" ' I will do my best,' " whispered Moppy.

" And is that an answer that Moppy would give from her heart?"

" Yes, Brown Owl."

" Then perhaps I may trust you with your Golden Hand," smiled Brown Owl. " For I know somebody who rates Moppy's best as very high indeed. There will be many eyes upon you, Moppy. Not only mine, but those of all the little folk who look to you for leadership. You won't fail us, will you?"

" I—I'll try not to," promised Moppy. " And thank you so very much, Brown Owl."

Then, like a puppy who is forgiven, she jumped from dejection to wild spirits.

" May I have it on the day Iris flies up?" she begged.

Brown Owl shook her head. Far too often did honour that should be Iris's have a way of attaching itself to Moppy. Though Moppy was to have her Golden Hand, yet it should be given quietly and seriously whilst she was still in a thoughtful mood about it. It should not be accompanied by a blaring of trumpets.

" If you show me an appetizing lettuce next Pack meeting, I will give you your Golden Hand the week after," she said.

CHAPTER XVI

Towards the Golden Ground

It was a Tuesday afternoon nearly three weeks later.

Betty was feeling just the least bit disgruntled. It was very ungrateful of her she knew, for it was so lovely being such friends with Moppy and Iris and Ann, and belonging to the Brownie Pack.

But it was Pack meeting time, and she had so hoped that by now she might have gone to some of the Brownie meetings and danced in the Fairy Ring that Moppy had described to her. If only she could have gone last week she would have seen Brown Owl give Moppy her Golden Hand. How she would have loved it!

There was the beautiful uniform that the Elf Six had given her lying all neatly wrapped in tissue paper with its brown shoes and stockings beside it, and she had never worn it except to try it on.

She knew her Brownie promise inside out, and had

been a Brownie for a good month, so she was quite
ready to be enrolled. She and Brown Owl and all the
Brownies so wanted it to happen at their Pack meeting.
But that tiresome doctor had said, " No; another
week or two!"

Then Mummie no longer went out charing, but she
was taking in more washing—the Pritchards had given
her theirs—and that made her very busy. And, of
course, it was lovely Daddie having work again; yet
he was such a kind Daddie that Betty had loved having
him in and out. She knew it was downright selfish
and silly of her, and that he was a much happier
Daddie now when he *was* in, but she was missing him
so very much during the day.

If it were only Wednesday she would not mind so
much, for she always felt so important on Wednesdays.
It was the day she did her extra special good turn and
ironed the hankies.

Mummie had long ago given up thinking that
Betty's helpfulness was just nonsense. Betty would
sit at the table and Mummie would bring her the hot
irons, and she would iron the handkerchiefs most
beautifully. She always especially loved doing those
of Iris and Ann.

Then suddenly Betty had an idea.

" Don't you think the hankies are ready for steaming?

I do want something to do, Mummie," she called out.

" I dare say," called back Mrs. Horpe from the scullery sink. " I'll put them in the bath towel and bring them in."

Betty smiled a serious little smile of satisfaction, and cleared the kitchen table for her job.

" There!" announced Mrs. Horpe, as she dumped them down. " Clever little girl!"

Betty spread them on the table and folded them in half with the little ones at the bottom in piles of twelve. Then she pressed them with a hot iron to make them dry enough for to-morrow's ironing.

Very tidily she put them back into the towel to wait.

She felt so grown-up and useful that she became hardly envious of the merry Brownie Pack. Then, just as she had folded the towel, she heard the postman's rat-tat.

The door was open and he came in.

" For the little 'un again," he laughed, and handed Betty a long thick envelope.

" It must be my July letter from Post Brown Owl," Betty cried. " Oh, I do wonder what it's like! Come and see, Mummie, quick!"

She tore open the envelope.

" It's written on pink paper. How pretty!" she

cried. " Three—no, four long sheets all clipped together. And whatever's that funny brown wedge
under the clip? Oh, dear, there's so much I want to
know!"

" My dear Brownie,

" I am sure you can sing the Brownie rhyme:
' We 're the Brownies, here 's our aim:
Lend a hand and play the game.'

But it's much more fun to sing it in a real Fairy
Ring, isn't it?"

" It is," sighed poor Betty.

" As you are not always able to go to Pack
meetings, I wonder if you would like to make
one of your very own?"

" Now, isn't that funny?" Betty told herself. " Just
after what I was thinking."

" All you have to do is to cut round the edge
of the Brownie——"

" Why, that must be the brown triangle under the
clip," thrilled Betty. " Oh! how exciting!"

" And then open it out. You will have a lovely
ring of dancing Brownies, but you must sing
the rhyme for them."

" Scissors, quick!" cried Betty, jigging up and down.

"Oh, yes, look! there's a little Brownie drawn in pencil. Isn't she a pet? Here she comes," she laughed as she snipped round with the scissors. "What fat little legs she's got! She looks rather like Ann.

"Now I'll open it out. Oo-er! there's six—no, they've stuck together here — eight duckie little Brownies all holding hands. Isn't my Post Brown Owl a darling to think of such a thing?"

"I do believe she tells you how to make them for yourself," smiled Mummie, peeping at the pink paper which had been laid down in the excitement of cutting out the Brownies.

"Does she? How lovely! Then I can make one for each of the Elves. Won't they be pleased?" cried Betty. "Let's see, Mummie!"

They laid the letter down on the table and looked together at Post Brown Owl's instructions.

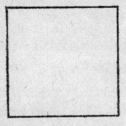

"Take a large square
of thin paper.

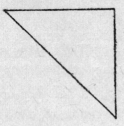

Fold it in half from
corner to corner.

then again   and again.   Now draw
your Brownie
and cut, but be careful not to cut the edge of the paper
where the hands come."

" There's the loveliest competition, too," cried
Betty, reading on. " It's all about a journey to the
Golden Ground. Listen!

> " If you have started on your journey to the
> Land of the Golden Ground, you will be able
> to fill in the blanks I have left in the story below."

A journey to the Golden Ground. How lovely that
sounded! Betty, who had never been for a journey in
all her life, to take one to the Golden Ground. Was
there ever any little girl so thrilled?

Now, of course, Betty had hardly started on her
journey for the Golden Ground, but Moppy had told
her so many of the milestones that she felt she need
not be completely lost if she puzzled her way to it.

" I think I'll get Moppy to help me and tell Post

Brown Owl when I write," she decided. " She won't
expect me to know much when I've only been a
Brownie such a teeny little time."

" Here comes Moppy," said Mrs. Horpe.

Sure enough here was Moppy waving in at the
window in full Brownie rig.

" Hulloa, Betty!" she cried, " I've just blown in
after Pack meeting. I sort of thought you'd wish you
were there."

" Thank you, Moppy. I want you dreadfully. I've
had my July letter from Post Brown Owl. Isn't it
funny you should come on the same day? You did
when I had my welcoming letter, you know. There's
a competition in it I want you to help me with. I
shall tell her, of course."

" Let's look," commanded Moppy. " I wish I was
a Post Brownie," she laughed, as she saw the pink
sheets. " I say, this sounds awfully nice!"

" Over the hills and far away lies the Land of
the Golden Ground. Would you like to go there?
I will tell you how a little Brownie called Vera
went there. She got her Brown Owl to go with
her and, if you are going, you will ask your Brown
Owl to go with you, won't you? Another Brownie
called Joan went too.

" They started off just at the time of the year when the leaves were all turning and the red berries were shining out of the dark hedges.

" The first town they came to was very exciting. It was called Union Jack town. They lost their way a bit there."

" So did I," softly laughed Betty. " But you and Brown Owl were good guides, Moppy. You soon made me find it."

" Some of the streets were wide and some narrow. It was so muddling."

" That came of halving St. Patrick," chuckled Moppy.

" And what do you think? Instead of policemen to show them the way there were three knights; great tall shining knights, with wonderful shirts on, each with a cross. Before they got out of the town Vera and Joan were great friends with them all three, but that was because they knew their names and lots about them. Their names were——"

" I know! I know! *Don't* tell," besought Betty. " St. George, St. Andrew, and St. Patrick."

" They soon left the town behind them, and

the road led by a little babbling brook. As the
sun was shining, and their frocks by this time
were rather grubby, they took them off and
washed them."

" I 'spect I'd do that better than either of them,"
declared Betty, who took everything in dead earnest.
" I think they were rather silly to do it, though, for,
of course, they couldn't iron them, and they'd look
horrid rough dried."

But such things did not worry Moppy. She would
have washed her frock too; just for the fun of it.

" Close by were two trees, and they tied a
rope between them. But, directly they put their
frocks on it to dry, down it slipped to the bottom
of the trunks, and they thought they would never
make it stay up, till at last Brown Owl showed
them a lovely way to do it with a——"

Betty stared vacantly at the blank, and even Moppy
looked doubtful.

" P'raps she used a clove-hitch," she said at last.

" Whilst their frocks were drying they ex-
plored the bank of the stream. Suddenly they
heard an animal rushing towards them, and round
the corner came a goat, dangling his lead. The
lead was a strap with a loop at the end.

" Quick as thought, Vera ran towards him. She caught hold of the lead and tied him up to a tree, using a bit of rope she had and fixing it to the loop with a——"

" Bother these knots," sighed Moppy. ' I expect it was a sheet-bend."

" Just then the farmer's boy, who had been in charge of the goat, came limping along the path. His knee was badly grazed, for he had fallen down when he had tried to catch the naughty goat. When the Brownies had——"

" Washed it," sang Betty.

" But perhaps the water wasn't clean," objected Moppy.

" Anyway, it was running water, and it was clean enough to wash their frocks, and it would be better than leaving the grit in," argued Betty.

" I suppose it would. But they *ought* to boil it, you know," objected Moppy, with the air of a grand-mother.

" When the Brownies had *washed* his knee," firmly continued Betty,

" they tied it up with a clean——"

" Bandage," rushed in Moppy. She really could not have her recruit thinking she knew best.

But here again she met with unexpected opposition.

" No!   Handkerchief," quietly over-ruled Betty. Not for nothing had she been steaming piles of hankies that afternoon. " I don't suppose they had a bandage with them."

" Well, they just ought to, if they were going on a long journey like that," maintained Moppy. She was in an unusually cautious mood that afternoon.

Betty ignored the alternative and went on reading.

" Fastening it with a——"

" Reef-knot," cried both the children in a dead-heat.

" He was so grateful, and, when they handed him back the goat, he couldn't thank them enough.

" They had lots of other adventures before they reached the Land of the Golden Ground, but these will have to wait for another time."

" Oh, I did want to get there," sighed Betty.

" Never mind, we shall be together at Urchin Bay when the August letter comes," reminded Moppy.

Then her glance fell on the ring of paper Brownies.

" Whatever's this?" she cried, taking it up.

" My Fairy Ring," smiled Betty. " Isn't it the loveliest thing? Post Brown Owl shows us how to make it. Look!"—and she pointed out the folded square.

" That's as easy as easy," laughed Moppy. " Let's each do one."

The children found their pencils. Mrs. Horpe lent a second pair of scissors, and then they both set to work.

" I've finished! You are a slow coach, Betty," cried Moppy, opening out her paper.

Then she gazed at it in disgust. " There's something wrong. The diagram can't have been right. All my Brownies are joined by their feet."

" The diagram's quite right," defended Betty. " Mine are all dancing properly." Then she looked at Moppy, and rippled with laughter.

" Yours do look queer! I see what you've done," she exclaimed. " You drew your Brownies' feet where the paper was doubled. But that's where their arms should come."

Moppy reddened. Again her pupil was forging ahead. Then she shook off her annoyance with a laugh. After all it was Betty's letter, and it was jolly nice that Betty should do the things in it better than she. But it was awfully funny when she had been so cocksure that she could do it. Brown Owl would laugh when she told her about the Brownies' feet. It would be a stolid dancing ring!

CHAPTER XVII

Betty's Enrolment

" I think I'm perfectly ready, don't you, Mummie?" asked Betty.

At last the doctor had said that Betty was well enough to go down to the Pack meeting and be enrolled. This time he had been kind, for his vague " week or two " really had been two, and not three weeks as Betty had feared. And here she was beautifully dressed in her Brownie uniform, her tie put on neatly enough even to satisfy the exacting Moppy who, however untidy she might occasionally be herself, was determined that no flaw should appear on her own Post Brownie. Her fair hair was literally shining from its brushing. The beret was just the right size. The leather belt gave the last touch to her spic-and-spanness.

The Rectory garden was a wee bit too far for even a very convalescent Post Brownie like Betty to walk to. The Pack had wanted to wheel her down in a bath chair, but Brown Owl had decided that the joltings

and erratic steerings and the squealings of excitement
that the Pack would give would not be over good for
Betty. So Mrs. Pritchard was driving her down. Mrs.
Horpe was coming too. She was dressed in her very
best, waiting with Betty for the car. As she heard it
draw up outside their little gate, she gave a despairing
look round her kitchen.

" Tuesday—my busiest day—and me leaving all my
washing! I think I must be daft," she cried. But she
gave Betty a good sounding kiss before they came
together out of the cottage door.

" There, duckie! you look fine," she pronounced,
pulling the fair hair forward under the beret.

Mrs. Pritchard whizzed them quickly down. " I'll
call for you when it's over," she reminded. " Good-
bye, Betty! You'll be a really truly Brownie when I
come back."

Betty smiled shyly at the kind lady who was so
like Iris; then she caught her breath in delight as she
saw all the Brownies scampering towards her over the
lawn.

How she was longing for them to form their Fairy
Ring and sing their rhymes! It was one thing to know
about everything and another to see and hear it with
one's own eyes and ears.

Elsie was to be enrolled that afternoon too. She

had been waiting on purpose. So Betty was not the only little brown-clad figure outside the Fairy Ring.

"Who are you, little Folk?" came Brown Owl's voice from within the ring.

"We're recruits," answered the wee voices of Elsie and Betty.

"What do you want, little Folk?"

"We want to be Brownies."

"Shall we let them?" Brown Owl questioned of her Fairy Ring.

"Yes!" cried the Brownies.

"Fetch them, Sixer," said Brown Owl to Iris.

Iris, eagerness shining all over her face, ran out of the ring and brought the would-be Elves to Brown Owl.

Then Betty saw quite close the toadstool totem with its dear little brown owl sitting on the top just as Moppy had described.

But Brown Owl was speaking to her.

"What is the Brownie law, Betty?"

"A Brownie gives in to the older folk. A Brownie does not give in to herself," whispered Betty.

"Do you know that if you now make the Promise you must always stick to it afterwards, and do your best to carry it out?"

"Yes," whispered Betty.

" Do you still wish to make it?"

" Yes."

" Come to the totem and repeat your Promise as a Brownie."

Very solemnly Betty stepped forward. Up went her right hand at the salute, while her left hand touched the totem. Then, fixing her big blue eyes on Brown Owl's face, she repeated her Brownie Promise in a voice that had suddenly grown so clear that not only was it heard by the Pack, but by Mrs. Horpe clasping her hands in nervousness outside the ring.

" I promise to do my best to do my duty to God and the King, and to keep the law of the Brownie Pack, and to help other people every day, especially those at home."

And then Betty saw the gleam of the Brownie brooch as Brown Owl pinned it on to her tie.

Then came the funny little blue Elf who was to live on his cloth background above her right pocket.

" You are now a Brownie," Brown Owl told her, " and wear the badge of the Elf Six. You must do your best at all times for the honour of your Six. Will you try?"

" Yes," breathed a radiant Betty, as she and Brown Owl saluted each other and shook hands, like the wonderful comrades they were, with the left hand.

There was the Pack to salute now, and there were her own thrilled Elves dancing with eagerness and beckoning her into their midst. She ran to them and seized the welcoming hands of Moppy and Ann. Iris was still anxiously watching over Elsie. She was so afraid she would forget her answers or burst out crying or do something not quite Brownie-like. But no, Elsie had been enough of a Brownie to do her best to learn her Promise, and she even summoned a tremulous little smile as, her enrolment over, she ran back and took her place in the Six between Iris and Bess.

And then more wonders took place, for the Pack was preparing to give its Grand Howl. Betty knew what to do, for she had been told all about it by her Brownie visitors. So she squatted on the grass with her two hands on the ground like all the other Brownies and joined with them in their slowly rising " Tu-whit, tu-who-oo-oo-oo!"

But she was quite unprepared for the piercingness of the final " Tu-whit, tu-who-oo-oo-o-o-O-O!" nor for the energy of the leap in the air and the clap of the hands that accompanied it. She was quite sure that it must have frightened away even the ghosts of the Boggarts.

Then came something for which no one had prepared her.

Mrs. Horpe was the only visitor, and Brown Owl did not intend her to spend one of her precious afternoons in forlorn state.

"Will you come into the middle of our Fairy Ring, please, Mrs. Horpe?" she called.

Mrs. Horpe started, reddened, and shook her head.

But somehow it was very difficult to refuse Brown Owl, and before she knew it, Mrs. Horpe found herself in that Fairy Ring looking nervously at the impish faces of the surrounding Brownies.

Then, horror of horrors, how could she ever have had truck with such nonsense? The Pack began to dance around her and sing.

" In the name of the Brownies we welcome you, we welcome
    you,
  In the name of the Brownies we welcome you.
  Shut your eyes——"

No, that she would not do! But whatever was coming over her? Bless me, if she hadn't done so!

" Shut your eyes and take a hand——"

And this she did too; she the wife of a respectable working man! Well, she'd give herself a good talking to when this was over, see if she didn't.

"——and we will lead you to Fairyland

There was a groping in the dark, and a tugging of eager little hands pushing and pulling her into their Fairy Ring.

And then just one voice—the voice of that naughty Brown Owl, who was grown up, and should have known better than to make a figure of fun of a hard-working woman.

> " Open now and you shall see what you shall see,
>   You shall hear what you shall hear, and
>   You shall know what you shall know."

And Mrs. Horpe did open them, all dazed and blinking in the sunlight, and bless us, if those little Brownies, looking more jiggy than ever after her shut eyes, didn't begin to dance round again taking her with them. And they were singing at her again, yes they were.

> " You are free to come and free to go,
>   To look and know what we shall show."

And then something, perhaps it was the Brownie magic, took hold of Mrs. Horpe, and instead of feeling like that little old woman who woke up and found her petticoats all cut about, she flung off all her present-day cares and became the jolly young girl that she had been not so many years ago after all; and she danced round with the children, and sang with them their rhyme, that she knew so well from hearing Betty sing it.

" We 're the Brownies, here 's our aim:
  Lend a hand and play the game."

And, after all, wasn't that her aim, although she never thought about it? Didn't she lend a hand when she could? Especially to those at home! And didn't she play the game? Though with her and Horpe lately the game had been that rather grim one of just paying one's way. Yes, there might have been a worse visitor to the Fairy Ring than Mrs. Horpe.

The Pack had decided at last week's pow-wow that every game it played to-day was to be one in which Betty could join. " Nice quiet ones, you know, Brown Owl, where we don't rush about," Moppy had said, with an air of a decorous grandmother. But it did not know that it was to be rewarded for its thoughtfulness by playing the most amusing game of all.

"Let's make a rice pudding!" announced Brown Owl.

The children hugged themselves with glee.

The loveliness of the Rice Pudding Game was a tradition with the Pack.

" I think my Golden Hand Brownie must help me cook," smiled Brown Owl. " Come along, Iris, and stand by me."

" The larder's over there," she explained, pointing to a long garden seat under a fir tree. " It's always nice and cool there.

" Now all you smaller Brownies run and put yourselves on the larder shelf, and take Betty with you."

Laughing their delight, the smallest Brownies surrounded Betty and ran with her to the seat.

" There's a cupboard there," continued Brown Owl, pointing to a may tree near. " And the sink is *there*," she added, looking towards a great bush of broom. " And the kitchen table's just in front of me."

" Please, Brown Owl, may I draw them?" begged Moppy, who was finding it very difficult to sit quietly on the grass while Iris was Brown Owl's right hand, and Betty and Ann were reposing in the larder.

" Very well."

So Moppy skipped from cupboard to sink, and from sink to larder, drawing imaginary lines in the air with the bold sweep of an artist.

" Please don't put a step to the larder," pleaded Brown Owl. " The architect did last time we made a rice pudding, and my kitchen maid didn't see it and kept ricking her ankle."

The Pack chuckled.

" And now my table."

Moppy drew a spacious table in front of Brown Owl.

" Now Iris, a pie-dish, please."

" A big one?" asked a deadly serious Iris.

" Rather!"

Iris took hold of Moppy, now retired from art, and led her to the kitchen table that she had just fashioned.

" Don't bring your pie-dish in bits," cried Brown Owl.

The Pack rippled its delight, and Iris ran round the ring of sitting Brownies, picking out the bigger ones and herding them in a bunch towards Brown Owl.

" That's better. It's an oval pie-dish, isn't it? Put it carefully down, and see there're no cracks in it."

Iris, in the manner of a careful housewife, arranged her pie-dish in front of Brown Owl. The delighted Brownies huddled close together to avoid cracks.

" Now the rice. How much do we want?"

" Enough to cover the bottom," sang the pie-dish.

So Iris ran to the larder and picked out several tiny Brownies to put at the bottom of the pie-dish.

" But you haven't washed the rice," cried a shocked Brown Owl.

" Oh dear!" cried Iris. She hurried her grains to the sink and gave them a most dramatic washing.

" Now the milk," anticipated the thrilled pie-dish.

So Iris ran to the cupboard and carefully chose a tall Brownie for her jug, then back to the larder where

Betty proved to be the milk, which was poured into the jug and solemnly put into the pudding.

" Sugar, Brown Owl!" cried one of the grains of rice.

" And butter!" shouted its neighbour.

" And nutmeg!" pleaded a portion of the pie-dish.

" And a pinch of salt!" reminded another.

So the sugar and butter and salt were added, and just a very little nutmeg was grated and sprinkled over the pudding. And all was ready for cooking.

Then Brown Owl and Iris moved the pie-dish very carefully and put it in the oven, but it was such a chattering, laughing dish, that Brown Owl declared that she thought she had got hold of the blackbird pie by mistake, at which the chirps and twitterings so redoubled that she became quite worried about the contents of the rice pudding.

" For how long must it cook?" she asked her assistant.

A grain of rice rather squashed and very anxious to move, chirped out " Twenty minutes " before Iris had time to answer.

But the rest of the pudding expressed its disapproval.

" I shouldn't like to get a twenty-minute rice pudding," laughed Brown Owl. " How long, Iris?"

" As long as you can give it in a slow oven, perhaps two hours," slowly replied Iris.

Brown Owl nodded. " If I had to have a Brownie to run my house for me, I should certainly choose Iris," she had once said. She was glad that Iris was justifying her choice.

Then she looked at Iris over the pie-dish and smiled mischievously. " As it takes so long to cook we'll just leave it there for a couple of hours and play a game by ourselves, shall we?" she asked.

" Let's," smiled back Iris.

Protesting groans arose from the oven.

" And then my father can have it for his supper."

Rather more violent and slightly frightened groans arose from the tiny grains of rice. Canon Chesney was very nice, but he did look rather grim when he wasn't smiling. Suppose he was an ogre and ate you?

" What a funny pudding! It doesn't want to be eaten," cried Brown Owl.

" No, we don't!" shrilled the pudding.

" Then—*Vanish!*" decreed Brown Owl, pointing her two first fingers at the rice pudding.

And lo, there was no pudding, but a Pack of Brownies rolling over one another in their efforts to straighten out.

When Mrs. Pritchard came back to fetch Betty and

Mrs. Horpe, Betty was just blue eyes and a Brownie smile. Never had she been so happy in her life.

But, as she waved her last good-bye to the waving Brownies, and leant back against the cushions of the car, she looked quite pinched with tiredness.

Mrs. Pritchard glanced at Mrs. Horpe. She knew what care she took of Betty, and was fearful lest Brown Owl and her Pack should be blamed.

But the Brownie magic must still have been working in Mrs. Horpe. " Of course she's tired," she admitted, answering Mrs. Pritchard's glance. " And I dare say being a Brownie at home is best for her most times at present. But it's been worth it! Betty'll be happy for many a week just thinking over the afternoon. And there's that visit to Urchin Bay coming along ever so quickly to set her up. My! she's a lucky girl!" exclaimed Mrs. Horpe.

CHAPTER XVIII

Iris Flies Up

It was the Saturday afternoon right at the end of July and the Rectory garden was very full. Brown Owl had invited to it both the Guide Company and the Brownie Pack, for it was the chosen day on which Iris was to fly up.

On the terrace in front of the house the Captain's whistle could be heard collecting her Guides, while on the lawn below Brown Owl was calling her Brownies into their Fairy Ring.

Very quickly all was made ready for the ceremony, and the Brownies stole shy glances at the Guides above them.

So smart were the Guides in their horseshoe formation, and so proudly were their Company colours borne in the centre—a golden trefoil on a royal blue ground—that it made all these little people feel particularly wee.

Iris herself was feeling rather choky and forlorn. She loved Brown Owl and the Pack so much and, fine though the Guide Company was, yet it was the unknown. Still, as Brown Owl had told her the night before, she was growing a big girl now, and she must not shirk the bigger things that older people are able to do. So, when the moment arrived for her to step forward and face Brown Owl by the totem, she came steadily enough, though her heart was beating so loudly that she thought that everybody must hear it.

" The time has come for you to take wings and fly up to the Company," said Brown Owl gently. " You have learned many things in the Pack; are you ready to learn more?"

" I am quite ready," replied Iris.

" Tu-whit, tu-whoo-oo-oo! Tu-whit, tu-whoo-oo-oo-oo!! Tu-whit, tu-whoo-oo-oo-oo-OO!!!"

Two pink patches stood out on Iris's cheeks, and her eyes became all starry and big.

It was the Grand Howl, and it was for her. It was the Pack's farewell.

" I will never forget I have been a Brownie," she told Brown Owl.

Indeed she would not—*ever*.

Brown Owl was holding the wings with which Iris was to fly up to the Guide Company.

" Now I give you Brownie wings
That you may fly to Guide-like things."

she said as she pinned them above the left pocket
of her uniform.

The Pack had still something to say to Iris before
she left it.

" Now it's time to say good-bye,
Open the ring and out you fly!"

it sang, and broke its Fairy Ring for just one moment
to release Iris.

She darted out and up the steps cut in the bank to
the waiting horseshoe. But, before she could enter
it, Cicely, her Patrol Leader, swung to meet her, and
held her arm across the empty space.

" Who goes there?" she challenged.

" A Brownie from the First Comfrey Hill Pack,"
answered Iris.

" By what right do you come?"

" By the right of my wings."

Then Cicely drew her into the horseshoe of smiling
friendly Guides, and led her to the Guide Captain,
who was waiting to welcome her with her left hand
outstretched.

Gravely Iris saluted the flag, and was received into
her patrol.

Of all the Brownies who were watching Iris fly up with such wide-open eyes there was none who was more thoughtful over it than the usually tempestuous Moppy.

She would be the next Brownie for whom the ring would break. Of course, being Moppy, she wanted to fly up, but she knew all of a sudden that she would hate to go. She would hate to leave all the little ones. Ann, who was holding her hand so tightly while she watched, that she was almost hurting. Betty—yes, it would mean leaving Betty, too. Tilda with her dimples and happiness. Even Elsie whom it was so difficult not to tease. Why, she loved them all, even when she over-rode them, and she would always love all the Brownie magic for their sakes. She felt that she would leave a part of herself behind in the Brownie Pack.

The thought followed her all through the rest of that afternoon. It prevented her quite enjoying either the jolly games that the Brownies and Guides played together afterwards, or the lovely tea that Brown Owl had provided.

The Brownies soon threw off their shyness of the Guides; indeed, had it not been for the thrill of the ceremony they would hardly have been shy of them at all, for they judged the Company by Madge, their Pack Leader. They all knew that it was quite impossible to feel Boggarty and shan't playish when Madge

was near them, and she always seemed to know just
what little fingers found most difficult about knots
and bandages and signalling. And if she was like that,
probably all those other jolly girls in blue were too,
so very soon most Brownies had annexed one particular big girl whom they wanted to play with, and
were pouring into her ears scraps of their favourite
Brownie lore.

" Let's show the Guides some of our singing games,
shall we?" suggested Brown Owl.

" Oh, yes!" chorused the Pack.

" Please, Brown Owl, may we have Three Bears?"
begged Tilda.

" No," demurred Elsie, who was a little frightened
of the realistic growls. " Do let's have ' I've come to
hire a housemaid '."

" We can have them both," compromised Brown
Owl, which pleased Tilda but not Elsie.

And so they did, and a lovely Rainy Day song too,
which the baby Brownies loved.

They sang it in a circle, and they acted every bit of
it, and rushed round and round when they were little
streams.

" Pit-pit-pit-pit," went fingers on to the palms of
hands; " patter-patter-pat," went their hands as they
clapped together.

" All the little raindrops come like that.
With our big umbrella open *so*,
We don't mind the raindrops, oh no! no!

" Pit, pit, pit, pit, patter patter pat,
All the little raindrops come like that.
Then the little seeds begin to grow,
They don't mind the raindrops, oh no! no!

" Pit, pit, pit, pit, patter patter pat,
All the little raindrops come like that.
All the thirsty flowers love them so,
They don't mind the raindrops, oh, no! no!

" Pit, pit, pit, pit, patter patter pat,
All the little raindrops come like that.
Then the pretty streams a-racing go,
They don't mind the raindrops, oh no! no!

" Pit, pit, pit, pit, patter patter pat,
All the little raindrops come like that.
Butterflies and bees are hiding—*so*,
They don't *like* the raindrops, oh no! no!" [1]

Then after tea they all sat round in the biggest pow-wow circle that any Brownie could imagine, and the Guides taught them some of their funniest songs and let them listen to the most beautiful.

[1] From *The Babies' Own Book of Song, Game, and Verse*, by Lucy M. Sidnell and Annie M. Gibbon.

Nobody wanted to go, and more than one Guide wondered why ever she had not asked to be a Pack Leader like Madge, so entrancing did they find these little people.

But the time to break up came at last, and, as it did so, Brown Owl drew near to Moppy. She had been noticing her quietness all the afternoon.

" What is it, Moppy?" she asked.

Moppy's eyes grew tragic.

" I shan't want to leave the Pack ever," she cried.

" Yes, you will," reassured Brown Owl. " Even now you're longing for bigger things. And perhaps you'll come back to us one day as Pack Leader."

Joy, amazement, and a sudden confusion chased each other over Moppy's face in one pink flush.

" Brown *Owl!* You can't think me worth it! You haven't made me a Sixer or a Second——"

" No. Because at present you're not a very wise Moppy. But the years will make you wiser," smiled Brown Owl.

CHAPTER XIX

Urchin Bay

" Pack Leader! Pack Leader!" Moppy made the words into a little inside chant as she began to get ready for her visit to Urchin Bay.

Wriggles might fill his kit-bag under her very nose for all she cared now. He might be going to camp, but he would never, she was sure, be Pack Leader, even if Wolf Cubs had such a personage, and she rather thought they hadn't.

Several times she was tempted to sing her chant out loud and tell everybody what Brown Owl had said, but a new humility kept preventing her.

But in every other way she was still anything but humble. She was quite certain that Betty could not get off without her help. She was so often round at the cottage suggesting this thing and that, that Mrs. Horpe had to whisk her away with a broom, and Iris had shyly to remind her that Betty would be their visitor, not Moppy's, and that if anyone helped Betty with her travelling trousseau, it really should be Mrs. Pritchard or Nannie.

At last the day came when they found themselves in charge of Nannie inside the reserved carriage that was to waft them to Urchin Bay.

Betty was comfortably ensconced in the corner seat that gave her the nicest view, and Moppy and Iris and Ann took it in turns to sit in the one opposite her. It was not often they had the chance of being with anyone who had never been in a train before.

" How big will the sea be?" asked Betty.

The children were at a loss to explain.

" It isn't *how* big. It's everywhere. It just goes on and on," attempted Moppy. " Urchin Bay's a lovely place, Betty. There's not only sea, there's river too. You couldn't have a better place to begin on."

" Couldn't I?" sighed Betty, bewildered with the attempt to take in the beauty through which she was whizzing, and the beauty to which she was to come.

And when she really got there and saw and heard the waves rippling over the sands, and sniffed the salt breeze, it was all so much finer than she had pictured that she was quite silent with joy.

" You shall bathe and paddle and lie on the sands and get brown all over," promised Moppy, who was again forgetting she was not Betty's hostess.

" And build the most lovely castles with tunnels and moats," put in Ann. " I'll get the water for you to fill your moat. But if you dig deep enough it fills itself," she explained.

During the rest of the day nothing seemed to matter except taking Betty right on to the sands and thinking of what the fortnight ahead of them would mean to her. But that night as Moppy lay in bed her thoughts flew off to Wriggles and his Wolf Cub camp.

When would they meet, she wondered? Possibly not very soon, for their camp was near a distant wood. Had Wriggles told the other Cubs they were coming and why? And was the Pack trembling for its prestige?

Moppy hoped it was, but in her heart of hearts she doubted. Akela was too resourceful and keen a Cub-master not to fill his Cubs' days right up with tracking and duties and bathing and sports. There would be very little time left over in which to think about even the most venturesome of little girls.

As a matter of fact, Wriggles' first night in camp had been rather a trembly one, although it was not the thought of the coming Moppy that had caused it to be so.

Almost the first discovery that the Cubs had made as they flung themselves out of their lorry and ran nelter-skelter around their camp site was that the wood at the back harboured snakes.

It was Cripps, the Senior Sixer, who discovered the first snake hole. Not long after a snake itself was seen. It was quite nine inches long.

" We must set snake traps round our tents, mustn't we, Akela?" exclaimed Cripps.

So some very hairy string was produced and pegged down.

" A snake hates the feel of it; it irritates him," explained Akela.

But all this talk about snakes was not very comforting for a nervous boy. Wriggles felt glad that Cripps was his Sixer. Cripps had brought a stick with him to camp. It was to make his tent behave, he said. Wriggles felt that even if a particularly dauntless snake were to pass the hairy string, it would not escape Cripps's bright eyes, and would be effectively dealt with by the big stick.

Then he remembered a hint that Akela had let drop before they started for camp.

When Pack meetings began again, one or two of the Cubs were going up into the Scout Troop. Akela had been carefully watching Wriggles. He did not think he would ever lead, though it was possible be might win for himself limitless courage in the far-off time of his vigil before he became a Rover. But it would be hard to find a Cub who was more loyal to his Sixer and his Pack. Perhaps in the autumn Wriggles might be made a Second.

Remembering this, he tried to banish `fear even from his thoughts. And after the first night the enchantment of camp so gripped him that it was jostled out all unconsciously.

CHAPTER XX

Three Unfortunates

" May we have a picnic on the sands to-day, Nannie?" pleaded Moppy, a few days after their arrival.

" Best stay in the garden," said Nannie. " You can get in the shade there. You can't on the shore. It's scorching. There's a terrible wind too, blowing off the sea. The sun and the wind would do Betty no good, and I've a lot of darning to get through. Iris and Ann wear twice as many holes in their socks and stockings when you're with them."

The wind certainly was high. It had nearly blown Moppy away when she had rushed down to the shore before breakfast. She quite agreed that it might be silly for Betty to battle against it.

" If Betty wasn't there wouldn't you trust us three by ourselves?" she wheedled.

Nannie shook her head.

" Not if we took Solomon with us?"

Nannie hesitated. Solomon was their black cocker spaniel. He could be as staid as Wisp was frisky.

Solomon's sedateness often worried Moppy. She never could realize it was only the habit of his breed that made him hold his tail horizontally instead of waving it aloft. She took it as a signal that joy was missing from his life.

But she had to admit that, as an escort, he was superior to poor left-at-home Wisp. Wisp would only have been an added danger to the trio, for he would certainly have engaged in a desperate fight that Moppy would have felt it her bounden duty to stop, however harrowing and bloody the job.

" Do let us go," pleaded Moppy. " We'll be as staid as Solomon himself."

" I wonder," smiled Nannie, as she consented. " Ask Mary to give you some eggs and fruit and sandwiches then, and don't forget dog biscuits and drink."

" Darling!" pronounced the trio. Mary, an apple-cheeked kitchen maid brought with them from Comfrey Hill, was promoted to cook while at Urchin Bay. She spent her days there in a beam of pride, and in successful attempts to please the children. There was no danger that she would be too busy to cut sandwiches.

" And if you're going, go quickly," continued Nannie.

Moppy stopped long enough to hug Nannie, to upset her work basket, which she left to Iris to pick up, and to tread on her best corn; then she rushed off to the kitchen.

" Give me bloater paste sandwiches, please, Mary," she begged. " And may I take three eggs from the egg-box? And please will you give us tumblers instead of mugs?"

" Why? They break much more easily," objected Iris.

Moppy's reply did not seem to fit in.

" We'll poach our eggs. I've always wanted to," she confided.

" Nannie meant us to have them hard boiled," said Iris. " She would never let us use the spirit lamp."

" I don't want to," chuckled Moppy. " I've a *much* better idea. The sun's just blazing, isn't it?"

" Yes," agreed Iris, pushing her hair from her hot forehead.

" We'll put the eggs in our tumblers and poach them in the sun. Glass attracts it, you know."

" Don't be silly!" laughed Iris.

" I'm not silly. Guides do it sometimes. Somebody told me. The sun has to be hot enough, that's all."

" I don't believe it, and Nannie meant hard boiled," persisted Iris.

Ann looked at Moppy with wide-open eyes. It sounded rather like magic, but then Moppy was always wonderful.

" Let's try," she exclaimed.

Two to one carried the vote, and a quarter of an hour later they gaily set out with shrimping-net and pails, and satchels slung on their backs.

They paddled and shrimped and looked for shells, but the wind was so strong that the powdery sand blew rattling round them, and the salt spray, as they leant over the rocks, made them very thirsty.

" Let's have our milk. It may turn sour if we keep it," conveniently suggested Moppy. And Iris liked the idea so much that she did not remind Moppy that it had been boiled.

" Lovely!" pronounced Ann, as she sat on a rock and quaffed. " I'm still thirsty, though," she regretted, as she drained her glass. " I suppose Solomon does want *all* the water we brought him?"

" Ann!" screamed a horrified Iris and Moppy.

" Can't we eat our greengages then?" coaxed Ann.

" Yes, let's!" seconded Moppy.

" Very well," permitted Iris.

The honeylike greengages made them quite fresh again, and for half an hour they busily shrimped.

At the end of that time Moppy flung down the net.

" I'm sure I've a ton of grit in my eyes," she exclaimed. " Let's go under the cliff and have dinner. It'll be sheltered there."

Alas, no! With the wind off the sea the remorseless sand just scurried after them. As soon as they opened a packet of sandwiches the sand showered upon them.

Solomon alone did not seem to mind the relish as he munched his biscuit.

" Let's poach our eggs," said Moppy.

The shells were cracked, and the eggs skilfully slithered into their tumblers. Slanting them to the rays of the sun the trio sat and waited.

The sun was hot enough to scorch their poor arms, but it seemed to have no effect upon the raw eggs reposing at the bottom of each glass.

" You mustn't be impatient," Moppy told a disbelieving Iris and a weary Ann. " The white'll soon set."

" I don't believe it will, and if it does, it'll be full of sand," wailed Iris.

" Oh dear!" sighed Ann, a little later.

In another five minutes even Moppy gave up hope.

" I'm afraid the eggs must want tropical sun," she announced.

Ann's face grew very long. " I wanted mine so," she faltered.

" You can have it all the same," valiantly declared Moppy. " Pretend it's an oyster and swallow it whole. It'll slip down like a toboggan."

Ann sadly shook her head.

" I *couldn't*. And I'm so hungry and so thirsty, and bread's such a stuffy thing."

" Just watch me," coaxed Moppy. She made a violent gulp and swallowed the egg well peppered with sand. " There! Easy as easy," she exclaimed.

But Ann had seen the wry face that Moppy had hoped she had hidden.

" I *couldn't*," she repeated more loudly than before.

And neither could Iris. Mournfully the two sisters tipped the spineless eggs from their tumblers and watched them disappear into the loose sand.

" Let's go for a bit of a walk then," suggested Moppy. " When you're really hungry you'll like the sandwiches."

Solomon was the only one of the party who enjoyed that walk. He had dined off his usual dog biscuits, and drunk the water that his mistresses had heroically given him, and now he was in excellent fettle for racing across the sands. He became nearly as puppyish as Wisp. There was no one visible from whom to protect his charges, so he threw sedateness to the winds, and lolloped along, his great silky ears flopping as he went, now chasing the spray, now leaping towards the many gulls that the high wind seemed to be bringing shoreward.

" I'm as hungry as a hunter," declared Moppy at last. " And both of you must be, too. Let's have the sandwiches now, even if we haven't anything to drink with them."

" All right," agreed a resigned Iris and Ann.

They undid their satchels and took out their packages.

And then an extraordinary thing happened. The smell of Moppy's bloater paste must have wafted straight to the hovering gulls. It suggested a delicacy the like of which they had never dreamed. They flew flapping around the children. Solomon leapt furiously, now here, now there, but they still circled just out of his reach.

" Oh! Oh! Oh!" screamed Ann.

Neither Iris nor Moppy was any braver. They flung their sandwiches from them and sprinted away.

So frightened were they that they ran on and on, never noticing where they were going.

Moppy, forging ahead, was the first to pull up. She was stopped in her flight by a sudden collision.

Looking up she saw Wriggles's Cubmaster towering above her. A host of Wolf Cubs were crowding round him. It was the first time they had met.

" Oh!" she groaned, as she caught the twinkle in Akela's eye.

" What's the matter this time? I can't see any bees," he teased.

But Moppy was far too breathless to answer.

The three flung themselves panting on the sands, while Solomon wriggled his hind half in appreciation of such stalwart reinforcements.

At last, secure and rested, Moppy raised a shamed face. " It was——"

" Something much bigger than bees," broke in Ann. She and Akela had become great friends over the binding of her leg.

" Gulls!" cried the trio in a dead-heat.

" They mobbed us," shuddered Iris.

" They wanted our sandwiches," explained Moppy.

" And they got them," sighed Ann. "And I am so empty inside."

" You couldn't do justice to our tea if you weren't," consoled Akela. " We were just going to have it on the shore."

CHAPTER XXI

Tea with the Wolf Cubs

" The Cubs will be frightfully bucked if you have tea with us. They like the unexpected; don't you, Cubs?" asked Akela.

The Pack looked a little doubtful.

This tea on the shore was a great treat, for the camp was too far off for it to happen more than once. They did not want anything to spoil its jolliness. Of course, as Akela said, they did want the unexpected to happen, but the unexpected they wanted was expected to lead to Cubby deeds of prowess like tackling mysterious strangers till they were caught red-handed in an act of crime, or finding gold watches and diamond necklaces on the sands and restoring them to distracted and overwhelmingly grateful owners. It was a very different and much less exciting good turn to share a tea brought down with difficulty on their own trekcart with three famished but well-nourished little girls whom they might see any day of the week at Comfrey Hill.

Besides, two of them had already received the Pack's good offices, and one at least had certainly not seemed overwhelmed with gratitude. Still, this one was Lorraine's sister, and Lorraine was such a decent chap, and so sure of his sister being a sport, that the Pack decided to put a good face on it.

Quickly the Cubs dug a trench in the sand and made their fire in it, while some unloaded the cart, and others scampered off with the special tea dixie to wangle water from the nearest cottage.

Moppy looked on enviously. For her Golden Hand Test she had laid and lit a fire at home. She would have loved to give suggestions and help, but the Cubs seemed perfectly able to do it without.

The tea was made in wonderfully quick time.

" We line up now with our mugs, and Akela ladles us out the tea," prompted Wriggles.

There was just one awkward moment when the trio produced their glasses.

"Why ever didn't you bring mugs?" demanded a Cub near by.

" 'Cos we didn't want to," retorted Moppy.

After that all was sheer bliss.

Not only the Cubs but the quartermaster too felt glad that his catering had been generous as he watched the ravenous children.

" Always told Akela that boys ate less than girls,"
he laughed.

At first the Pack was a little shy of Iris and Moppy
and Ann. But tea and the fire and the jolliness of it
all soon thawed them.

Wriggles sat next to Moppy. Even before the Pack
thawed he was stammering out his news.

" The porridge is lovely," he told her. " We roast
in *our* camp! We have eggs and bacon sometimes,
and sometimes p-pineapple chunks. We had a large pot
of pickled cabbage yesterday. It was gone in a minute."

Next to Wriggles sat Cripps, the Senior Sixer. He
was an alert little fellow, smaller than many of the
boys he ruled. There was something pointed about his
whole appearance, and he had a way of sitting upright
on his haunches which made him look curiously like
a young wolf. Two gold stars were twinkling either
side of the wolf's head on his cap. He was, of course,
a two-star Cub, with both eyes very wide open.

" He's our detective," the Cubs volunteered.

" His dad lost a bob once," explained a rosy-cheeked
Cub, peeping at Moppy round Ann. " He was storm-
ing the place down, and Cripps discovered it for him
in the hem of his trousers."

" He found a tramp once among the raspberries,"
announced another.

" He was just going to turn his hose on him," shrilled a third.

" But that was his uncle in his gardening clothes," shouted the Pack.

One boy only did not join heartily in the merriment. He seemed a little uncomfortable.

" What's the matter with that boy over there?" Moppy asked Wriggles.

Wriggles did not answer.

Another Cub, sandy and garrulous, had no qualms.

" He disobeyed orders," he whispered. " So we stripped him and flung him in the nettles."

" Oh!" said Moppy thoughtfully. But the flood of chatter soon made her forget the woeful tale.

" Bet you girls can't cook potatoes like we do them," grinned the camp epicure. " Want to know how?"

" *Um-m*," stressed Moppy. Iris smiled, and Ann beamed a similar desire.

" You get some clay and pour cold water on it and smash it up into bits and make it all soft."

" Messy," demurred Moppy, wrinkling up her nose.

" You wrap it round the potato and put it under the ashes and hide it right up. It's done in ten minutes. Some people wouldn't dare eat it, I know. But it's topping!"

" We acted a play last night," announced Cripps, whose mind soared higher than food.

" The doleful-drama-of-the-dreadful-death-of-the-Duchess-of-Dulwich," chanted the Pack. "*Fine!*"

" There are t-two in a wood," explained Wriggles.

" You knock a man on the head," interposed Cripps.

" Knock him *flat*," emphasized the sandy one.

" You take a girl into a great big tower. I was the girl," shrilled the smallest Cub.

" A *burglar* comes," thrilled Cripps.

" He's counting the jewels!" supplied rosy face.

" He stabs her!" gloated the sandy one.

" He t-takes the jewels and runs away," took up Wriggles.

" A detective with a dog tries to catch her," cried another.

" He gets knocked out," stated the Pack.

" There's a second detective, and the *robber* gets knocked out," continued rosy face.

" I'm *that* detective," boasted Cripps.

Moppy was very silent as, at the bidding of time and Akela, they tore themselves away from the rollicking Pack and went off home along the sands. One thing was certain. Her self-respect demanded it. She must be a detective.

At last she deigned to tell Iris and Ann of her great idea.

" Daddie says the greatest detectives at Scotland Yard are called The Big Four. We might be the Thrilling Three," she conceded. " No! We can be a Big Four too, for Betty can detect when it's near home."

Iris and Ann shivered. Even thinking about detectives made them feel creepy.

" There's a magnifying glass in the sitting-room, isn't there?" remembered Moppy. " We'd better keep it by us. It may come in very useful. We shall have lots of things to learn if we detect. Detectives go to school, you know."

" Aren't you mixing them up with pickpockets?" asked Iris. " They do. Daddie told me they have to pick the pockets of a figure that is covered with bells without ringing a single bell."

But Moppy was for the moment ranged on the side of righteousness. She disdained to hear of the habits of pickpockets.

" I think you're silly, then," unexpectedly retorted Iris. " Daddie says it never does to under-rate your enemy."

CHAPTER XXII

A Chapter of Accidents

The magnifying glass had very little rest during the next two days. Neither had Iris nor Betty nor Ann. Moppy kept chivvying them here and there to decide whether various footmarks were those of Solomon or Mary or Josephus, the cat, or only those of some friendly ducks that occasionally waddled into their garden with many bows.

" Well, you can't be detectives without studying," Moppy would declare whenever they showed signs of rebellion.

Betty enjoyed using the magnifying glass in the house best. One did not have to go on all fours to examine prints like one did when investigating footmarks. And it was great fun to see the tiniest eye-squeezing print grow black and bold under the powerful glass.

Then after dinner on the second day, just as Moppy had strewn the sitting-room with every available paper and the worst printed books she could find, Mary put her head in at the wide-open window to say that if they came at once, Jim, an old fisherman friend, would take them out in his boat while he went to have a look at his lobster pots.

" We'll come," cried Moppy, leaning out of the window. She cast the papers she was holding on to the broad sill and flung the magnifying glass upon them. " Bother, though, Betty can't. It's her resting-time. Be all right on the veranda, Bet? Come on, you two."

" We've left everything about," protested Iris.

" What does it matter? We can tidy later. It's much more important to see those lobster pots," disposed Moppy.

About an hour afterwards Betty looked up from her reading to see Wriggles come whistling through the gate.

" Hulloa, Betty," he greeted.

" Hulloa," smiled Betty.

Wriggles ran up to her and stood shyly by her chair. He was awfully interested in Betty, but he had not seen her very often, and never alone. It was jolly to find her cheeks quite brown.

" You l-look ever so much better," he exclaimed.

" I'm almost well," triumphed Betty.

" To-morrow's our last day in camp, worse luck," sighed Wriggles. " You're awfully lucky to be staying longer. Akela's given us a free day so that he can get on with the clearing up. Quarter's taking most of the Cubs for an outing. They're going to buy presents to take home. But Cripps and I stayed behind and helped this morning, and now I've come over to Moppy."

" She's gone out in a boat, but she won't be long," explained Betty.

" *Hulloa!*" Wriggles started, then he bit his lip and grew very red and jerky.

" What's the matter?" asked Betty.

" N-nothing," stammered Wriggles. " W-why don't you go the other side of the veranda in the shade?" he asked with strange urgency. " It's b-blazing here."

" I'm all right," smiled Betty.

" I—I want you to," jerked Wriggles. " P-please d-don't ask why."

Betty stared. But there was something in Wriggles's face made her go. He so desperately wanted her to.

After all, a Brownie promises to obey and, although Wriggles was not one of the older folk, he just made Betty feel she must.

Once rid of Betty, Wriggles darted across the

veranda. Through the sitting-room window smoke was pouring. It was that that had caught his eye a moment ago. His first instinct had been to cry out. He had remembered just in time how bad a shock might be for Betty. It had seemed dreadful to be wasting time, but he just had to get her away.

There was a butt of water in the garden and a pail by it.

Wriggles flew to the butt, plunged the pail in, and dashed up to the window. The fierce sun, concentrating itself upon Moppy's magnifying glass, had set fire to the sheaf of papers beneath, and the flame was now running up the curtains. Wriggles overturned his pail upon the blazing mass, then he gripped a curtain just above the blaze. It came tumbling down, bringing the pole with it. The end of the pole jerked through the glass and smashed it into splinters.

The sound of breaking glass must have echoed through the house. It brought Nannie and Mary running to the spot.

" Oh!" they cried. But neither lost her head.

Nannie seized a rug and smothered the blazing sill. Mary threw the tablecloth over the remaining curtain and crumpled it in her arms.

Then they looked outside the window.

A shaky little Wolf Cub stood with twitching face

gazing down at his snatched curtain now blazing un-disturbed on the gravel walk.

Nannie suddenly realized how the pole had fallen.

With a little motherly cry, only kept for very rare moments, she rushed to him and gathered him into her arms as if he had been a baby.

" Come, dearie, cry it out," she crooned, as she took him with her into her very own sanctum.

" I wonder how it happened," mused Mary.

Moppy did not wonder when she returned home half an hour later.

She had a vivid memory of the magnifying glass on the sill, and not all her failure with poaching eggs had shaken her in her belief of the power of the sun's rays.

" It's my fault," she calmly told Nannie. Then she waited for the storm to break.

But it was not a very violent storm. Nannie did not believe in crying too much over spilt milk, and the thought of the disaster that might have been and wasn't, made her too grateful to be furious. Besides, as Moppy stood there upright and white, for she did not lack imagination, and could picture with Nannie the might-have-beens, she looked for the first time in her life rather like the little figure that Nannie had (a dead secret, of course) been cuddling in her lap a bare half-hour ago. And for the sake of the quivering Wriggles she forgave. " Poor little girl! It'll be a long time before that's out of her mind," she pitied. But here she was wrong.

Moppy was desperately sorry. But she was also terribly injured in her pride. Yet another plan of hers had led to disaster. Even by tea-time she was beginning to brood over some fresh way to glory. Suddenly there flashed into her mind the thought of an old deserted water-mill that stood on the river bank not very far from Wriggles's camp. It seemed to promise adventure.

" May I walk back with Wriggles?" she asked.

Nannie nodded. The brother and sister would probably like to be alone, she thought, after the disaster in which they had both played such different parts.

" Iris and I will come and meet you on your way back," she said.

But it was water, not fire, that was filling Moppy's mind as they started on their inland walk.

" Let's go by the mill, Wriggles," she cried. " I passed it once. It's all gloomy and haunted looking. I 'spect if anyone wanted to hide that's where they'd go, don't you? Do you think we shall have any luck and find someone slinking in the shadows?"

Wriggles hoped not. There still seemed to be a

smell of singeing about his jersey; the flame had licked the sleeve as he had clutched the curtain. He had had enough of derring-do for one day.

As they reached the water meadows through which the river wound on its way to the mill, everything looked so beautiful, bathed in the gold of the evening sun, and the river was flowing so gently through banks fringed with reeds and bulrushes, with here and there a patch of water forget-me-nots peeping vividly through, that Wriggles's spirits rose, for it did not seem possible that anything lurid could await them amidst such loveliness.

Soon everything was made still more beautiful by the swirling of falling water. For, although the mill wheel was no longer active, yet just by it there were still remaining old-time sluices through which the water foamed and tumbled into a pool below.

A bend of the river soon brought them within sight of the grey stone-built mill. Moppy dragged Wriggles to it, and made him peer with her into its desolate barnlike inside. It seemed a store-house for cob-webs and broken disused iron. There was nothing romantic now about the old mill, whose great wheel used to revolve so musically round and round. Nor did there seem to be within any hider from his fellow-men.

Moppy turned dejectedly away.

She ran over the brick pathway that bridged the river, and turned for comfort to the old sluices. She and Wriggles stood looking down at the whirling water, liking the noise and movement.

Across the sluice were wooden planks.

" Let's walk on them," Moppy exclaimed.

Wriggles shook his head. " Akela took us here the other day. He told us not to."

" Cowardy—cowardy—custard," laughed Moppy, as she hopped on to one of the planks and ran gaily along it.

The next moment there was a cry instead of a song.

Moppy's foot had slipped and she had tumbled down the bricked sides of the sluice into the foaming water.

In a dry summer like this the water was quite shallow, but Wriggles did not realize this, and Moppy had knocked her head as she fell. For the moment she was stunned. She was, therefore, in danger, however shallow the water might be.

At the lower end of the sluice, half-way down the wall, was a looped chain.

Here and there above it a missing brick gave a hold for foot or hand. If one were limpetlike enough it was possible to slither down to the chain.

Scraping along the side of the wall Wriggles reached it and clutched. He hung clinging to it and stretched out for Moppy with his other hand.

He managed to grip her shoulder as the water pushed her towards him. Then he waited while his brain thudded with thoughts.

Akela's distress if anything happened. . . . Akela responsible for the Cubs. . . . Akela putting them on their honour to avoid unnecessary danger. . . . Moppy must not drown. . . . *Moppy must not drown.* . . . Akela. Moppy. Moppy. Akela. So they hammered themselves out.

And it was all but for a moment. A man cycling by with his two schoolboy sons had heard Moppy's cry. The three had turned round at once and come racing back.

It was easy work to lower the younger boy and haul up the two children.

Upon seeing Wriggles's terrified face the man was careful to laugh off even the thought of an earlier danger.

" A bit circumscribed and noisy down there, but one could paddle in the water, sonnie," he laughed. " And your sister's opening her eyes now. She'll be cheeking us in a minute! Once she's herself I'll get her to slip on my coat."

He was not far wrong in his joking estimate of Moppy.

" Goody! what are you all staring at?" was her first remark.

Then she saw the fright in Wriggles's eyes and passed her hand over her forehead.

The colour flowed back into her face a little more vividly than it need have done.

" Oh, I remember. I slipped," she said very quietly.

" Think you could sit tight on the carrier while I run you home on my bike?" asked the man.

" Rather!" said Moppy, with almost her usual smile.

The elder boy took Wriggles on his step, and it was thus that Nannie and Iris met them just as they had started off for their walk.

Nannie was so worried when she heard about it that she was far angrier than she had been about the fire. She did not like the sound of concussion, and she was beginning to think that this charge of Moppy was more than she cared to tackle.

" You go to bed and wait there while I fetch the doctor to you," she told Moppy. Then her eyes fell on Wriggles's anxious face, and she smiled.

" Your sister's sent to bed for naughtiness and nothing else," she told him. " And I'm having the doctor to frighten her into goodness. So no worrying, please. But you can stay until he's been, and I'll ask him to drive you back to camp in his car."

The doctor's verdict was quite a comfortable one.

" She's had slight concussion, of course," he confirmed. " But the knock was not serious. Still, keep her in bed to-morrow. It's always best to be quiet for a bit if there's been any unconsciousness from a blow on the head."

Wriggles crept in to say good night to Moppy before going back to camp.

" Good-bye, Moppy. Wish we weren't going off to-morrow and leaving you in bed," he said wistfully.

Moppy coloured. She knew it would spoil his last evening in camp.

" Sorry, Wriggles," she said a little huskily. " My love to Mum and Dad, and tell them I really will be like Solomon for the rest of the visit."

CHAPTER XXIII

The August Letter

" May I come in?" asked Betty, putting her fair head round Moppy's bedroom door.

" *Rather!*" welcomed Moppy.

Betty tiptoed in after the manner of the most careful nurse, and put a chair so that she should sit well in view. She knew from experience how tiresome it was when people would sit so that you had to screw round to see them.

But Moppy's face looked so round and glowing, framed by the whiteness of the pillows, that there hardly seemed any need to tiptoe.

Except for a headache the night before, Moppy certainly did seem none the worse for yesterday, but nurse was following the doctor's order and keeping her very quiet.

She had thought Betty an excellent visitor to send. But Nannie had reckoned without the long envelope that Betty was gripping.

" Moppy, look!" she exclaimed. " My August letter's come. It's on blue paper this time. I've been longing to show it you all through breakfast. Isn't it funny me reading it to you in bed?"

It certainly did seem to be turning the tables. And, as there was nothing serious about the turning, both Moppy and Betty dimpled over it as an excellent joke.

" It goes on about the Land of the Golden Ground, doesn't it?" asked Moppy.

" Yes, and there's a lovely drawing of it. Look!" cried Betty, opening out the sheets. "See! It's like a map. There's the land all golden in the distance, and there're blue mountains and a forest in front of them, and there's a clearing in the forest with Union Jack town in it. Isn't it fun?"

" Um-m," admired Moppy. " Let's see what Vera and Joan do next."

" I will read it you," announced Betty, remembering once more that she was a nurse.

Moppy sighed. She could read it in a twinkling herself, and Betty was slow at reading aloud. Still, even madcap Moppy could not help knowing what a lovely feeling it must be for Betty, the invalid, to be sitting so importantly on a chair by someone else's bedside. She would not spoil Betty's game of nurse by butting in.

" When Vera and Joan and their Brown Owl had said good-bye to the boy and the goat, they started off again on their journey. Round the bend in the path the trees got thicker and very soon they found they were in a little wood. Presently they saw blue smoke curling up through the branches, and suddenly the trees parted and there in a little clearing was the prettiest wee house you ever saw.

" As they passed the door they heard someone crying inside, so Brown Owl knocked at the door and a voice said, ' Come in '. Brown Owl opened the door and put her head in, and there she found a dear little old lady sitting in a rocking-chair before the empty hearth, sobbing and moaning as she rocked herself gently to and fro.

" After a bit she told Brown Owl what was the matter. Her little grandchild who lived with her had just been taken away to the hospital to have an operation, and she had been up nights nursing her, and she was *so* tired, and her head ached *so* much, and she was *so* sad because her little Margaret was so ill.

" Brown Owl tried to comfort her, and as she sat talking to her she looked round the room. The window was tightly shut,"

" How dreadful!" murmured a shocked Moppy.

   " and there were cobwebs over it. The dresser was thick with dust, and the cups and saucers so dirty. There were some dead flowers in a vase on the mantelpiece, and on the table were the remains of the last meal.

   " The little old lady saw Brown Owl looking, and she said, ' You are thinking how dirty and untidy my room is. I am so ashamed that you should see it like this, for I always keep it nice, but since Margaret has been ill, I have been too tired and sad to see to it.'

   " ' Never mind,' said Brown Owl, ' let us see what we can do.' So she called in Vera and Joan, and said, ' Come on, Brownies, let's make this little old lady really and truly happy and comfy.'

   " So they set about it with a will. What do you think they did to that room? Can you guess?"

" There was *crowds* to do," chuckled Moppy, who could keep quiet no longer, and was always at her best when a rush was on. " They would open the window first, of course; wide top and bottom. Ugh! It must have been shut for ages if there were cobwebs on it!"

" But the old lady mustn't be in a draught," ob-

to get her dinner ready. And what did they do for that?"

" I do hope the old lady hadn't a large appetite. There wouldn't be much time to make a rice pudding, would there? But they could boil an egg and make some toast and a cup of tea. P'raps that would be solid enough for an old woman. And there might be some fruit in the garden. Mightn't there? Anyway, there'd be blackberries in the wood."

" Blackberries aren't good for an old lady," objected Betty, the authority.

" Oh! well, she must do with egg and tea and toast just for once," disposed Moppy a little heartlessly. " There's still something else for them to do. Look!"

' And then they found the little old lady's work-basket with a whole *heap* of stockings in it, and *there was a hole in every one!* So what do you think they did with them?"

" Darned them and did them up beautifully in pairs," cried Betty.

" Poor Brownies!" sighed Moppy, who hated darning.

" But listen to what comes next," cried Betty, who had now regained her letter.

"When they had done everything they could, and were ready to leave, the old lady was all smiles and happiness. So were they when she told them that the Land of the Golden Ground was just through the wood, ten minutes' walk away.

"Very soon after that they arrived, and oh! what a welcome they had! There were dozens and dozens of Brownies there, and they all asked questions at once: 'When did you start?' 'How did you come?' 'Did you have any adventures?' till Vera and Joan were quite bewildered.

"Suddenly Brown Owl said, 'Come along, you must have your badges now,'' and she led them along to the Hall of the Totem, and there in the presence of all the other Brownies she gave them their badges, the badge of the Golden Ground.''

"You'd be one of the Brownies who'd be there to welcome them, wouldn't you, Moppy?"

But Moppy was silent. Somehow the picture of Joan, happily washing up all alone at the sink, would stick in her mind. Betty had thought it would be quite all right. And Betty would have done it, she was sure. Iris would, too. And Ann would have tried, mounted on a wooden stool and making herself very wet. But

Moppy simply could not imagine herself at that sink at all. It was the exciting things that she liked to do, with everybody looking on and saying, "What a wonderful Moppy!" And what holes she put people into when she headed for these excitements! And how different the Urchin Bay visit had turned out from what she had planned. Lovely, of course, in spite of starvation, and a charred window-sill, and knocks on the head. But different. She had certainly not shown the Wolf Cubs what splendiferous things girls could do. She just seemed to have failed each time. But, even if she had succeeded, would she have been a better Brownie than Vera and Joan of Post Brown Owl's letter? Of course she wouldn't. And they had reached the Golden Land just by doing dull things that anyone could find to do anywhere. Only sometimes one was careful not to look for them.

"You'd be there to welcome them, wouldn't you, Moppy?" repeated Betty, surprised by her long silence.

"I don't believe I ought to be," was the amazing answer of this cocksure Brownie.